I0534541

The Mists of Time

Also by David C Arkless

The Secret War: Dhofar 1971 – 1972

First Published in 1988 by
William Kimber & Co Limited

Second Edition Published 2015 by
Reiver Publishing

The Mist of Time

David C Arkless

Reiver Publishing
Scotland

MMXIX

This novel is entirely a work of fiction. The names, characters and incidents portrayed in it are the work of the author's imagination. Any resemblance to actual persons, living or dead or localities is entirely coincidental. In order to add authenticity to the story there are exceptions to the above statement: where the Royal family or members of the Royal Family are mentioned. However where actions by the Royals or Royal Decrees supposedly by them are mentioned these are purely fictitious creations by the author and in no circumstances should be attributed to any member of the Royal Family.

The Mists of Time
Published 2019 by
REIVER PUBLISHING
©

David C Arkless, 2019
ISBN 978-0-9929339-3-7

*

*

*

A CIP catalogue record for this book is available from the British Library

For My
   Friends and Family

Contents

Birth is but a sleep and a forgetting
(William Wordsworth 1770-1850)

Preface

Humans are curious by nature and are for ever seeking answers to a variety of subjects. But perhaps there are two questions that have been asked over the centuries that have never been fully answered to everyone's satisfaction.

The first of these is what happens to us when we die? Many believe that nothing happens, that the end of life is just that, a finish of who you are. But what if it is not? What becomes of your inner self, your spirit your soul that defines who and what you are and is not part of your earthly trapped body. Does that also die? What if it leaves your body at the time of death, similarly to when it enters the body before birth and joins with your physical self? If this is the case then where does it come from and where does it go?

What if there are other parallel worlds that exist alongside ours but in a different time zone or dimension than the one we presently live in? Does the spirit travel to these or is there a timeless world that we enter to live in limbo until we are called upon to re-enter this world again.

The second question that may well be related to the above is that of Time. Time to some can mean many things. It can be the time of the day or the time of the bus or train that we catch to work each morning; it can be the time of our last holiday; it can be 'the time of our life'; it can be many things. So time can have many aspects and represents many different things to different people. But time itself can be difficult to define.
Time is with us as a past, a present and we hope a future. We cannot taste it or feel it or hear it but it exists and we all recognize that. Without time, the world as we know it would be a chaotic

ix

place. We organize ourselves with time. Time is a dimension but unlike other dimensions it can only travel in one direction and that is forwards, not backwards or to the right or to the left, but what if it could?

Throughout the centuries man has tried to define time. The Greek philosopher Aristotle concluded that time must be eternal while in later years scholars of different religions argued against that belief. So does time have a beginning and an end and if so what was before time began: more importantly what will happen if time ends?

Over the years there has been much debate amongst philosophers and scientists if time travel is possible. Einstein's Theory of Relativity certainly indicates that it is achievable. Many of today's physicists continue to study not only whether it may be possible but also how it could be done.

So what if there are other time zones or dimensions that exist alongside ours with people leading similar lives as we do? If the answer is yes then just imagine if we could pass into these other zones? What would we find? Would we find solutions to some of the global situations faced in our world of today or would it present us with bigger problems?

Perhaps time will tell.

The Mists of Time

Part 1
Chapter 1

Fugitives

It was a dark night made worse by the low rain clouds that only briefly allowed the light from a weak moon to filter through occasional gaps in the clouds. The two riders wrapped tightly in long cloaks, their wide brimmed felt hats pulled down tightly on their heads that were lowered against the wind driven rain, allowed the horses to make their own way along the muddy track.

They had been riding most of the night without let-up and both riders and horses needed to rest but the thought of their pursuers getting ever closer and the fate that awaited them if they were taken kept them going.

The year was 1645 and the riders were fleeing from the disaster suffered by King Charles I and his Royalist army that would become known as the Battle of Naseby.

The victors, Oliver Cromwell's model army, were giving no quarter to those that had survived the battle and who were now being ruthlessly hunted down.

The two riders, Alan Horsley and Daniel Colbert, were both from the town of Hexham a small market town in the north of England. Daniel's family were involved in producing leather goods and clothing in a growing market and had recently developed connections for the sale of their goods in Newcastle.

Daniel stood at five feet eight inches, was fair-haired and at twenty-eight years old just two years older than his companion. Daniel was married with a three-year-old daughter, Elizabeth, and although his wife had not yet told him she suspected that she was carrying a second child. His wife Denise was actively involved with the family business, stitching various articles of clothing and helping to train younger girls in her skills.

After Daniel's mother died his father had moved in to live with them and it was expected that Daniel would eventually take over the running of the business, but events about to take place would change their plans.

Daniel's companion, Alan Horsley, stood four inches taller than his friend at six feet of solid muscle developed from long days spent working in his father's forge making tools, farm implements and shoeing horses. He often accompanied Daniel when he visited Newcastle where the two of them would enjoy the freedom from family restraints. It was during one of these visits that they heard the call from William Cavendish Marquis of Newcastle, to join his Newcastle Regiment of Foote in support of the King.

 The two friends had grown up together and were strong supporters of the King as were their families and most of their neighbours. When the call came for loyal supporters to join the Royalist army they had not hesitated. Although their families did not want them to leave they knew that it was their duty to go so they made sure they were prepared with everything they might need for their journey.

Daniel's father had provided them with two fine horses, blankets and clothing while Alan's father gave them the best swords in his foundry and a pair of flintlock pistols each. It was not just the opportunity for excitement as young men that stirred their blood but a strong desire to serve the King against those who would do him harm.

The pair travelled to Newcastle and joined the Troop of Horse that was part of the Marquis's Regiment. Over the next few years they took part in various skirmishes in the northern half of the country until eventually they attached themselves to the King's army as part of Prince Rupert's Lifeguard of Horse and became involved in the cavalry charge at Naseby that ended in disaster.

It had come about after the Royalists army having routed the town of Leicester was travelling north to join up with their Scottish Royalist allies under the Marquees of Montrose. The new model army led by Oliver Cromwell and Sir Thomas Fairfax gave pursuit after lifting their siege of Oxford. The Royalists travelled more slowly than the Parliamentarian army and being unable to outdistance themselves and not wanting to be attacked from the rear were forced to stand and fight. It was on a misty June morning near the village of Naseby that the two armies faced themselves over rolling grasslands.

During the battle the King had given the order to his cavalry to charge and led the charge himself from the front. One of the King's aides, a Scottish nobleman, fearing that the King would be killed had grasped the reigns of his horse and led him away to safety. The other horsemen seeing the King turn hesitated and broke away from the charge. This gave the Roundhead army the opportunity to regroup and swiftly advance to break the Royalists. Many threw down their arms and asked for quarter but most were slaughtered where they stood including some unarmed women travelling with the baggage wagons.

The two friends had fought valiantly against the Roundhead army; close quarter fighting was the order of the day. It was during one of the wild charges that Daniel had narrowly missed a fatal blow from a sword wielded by one of the Roundhead officers. He was only saved as his horse stumbled on the uneven ground and the intended blow sliced through thin air.

He saw the disappointment on his antagonist face as they were driven apart by the confusion of battle. Daniel waved and laughed at him before saluting him with his sword and then he concentrated on the fight around him. But as the Roundheads gained the upper hand it made sense to leave the Battle field and fight another day rather than be taken prisoner or slaughtered without mercy.

As the two friends rode off they were spotted by a troop of Roundhead cavalry who immediately gave chase. They had managed to avoid their pursuers by hiding in a wood and watching as they rode past, now, as night fell they gained some respite from the chase in the blanket of darkness. Only allowing their horses to stop to drink from streams they kept moving so as to put as many miles as possible between the Roundheads and themselves. By luck and the poor weather they had managed so far to keep ahead of the Roundheads, but the question was for how long?

After a while the rain began to ease and the wind dropped as the sky began to fill with the light of dawn. This increased the possibility of being spotted by their pursuers but thankfully as they entered a forest the morning mists given off by the foliage thickened and cloaked their progress helping them on their way.

The track wound its way through the tall closely stacked trees that only allowed a small amount of light to filter through from above. Before long they came upon a fork in the track and observing by the amount of hoof marks and wheel ruts that the left hand path was mostly used they choose that one. After a short distance they turned off to their right and made their way through the trees and once out of sight of the track dismounted. While Daniel held the horses reigns, Alan returned the where they had left the track and carefully covered any sign of their exit. Satisfied they proceeded through the trees until they reached the less used track and remounting the horses carried on with their journey. They soon came to a wide stream and deciding to take further measures to hide their tracks began to wade downstream through the gently flowing waters.

Eventually the stream began to widen and soon they heard the gentle sound of surf of a receding tide as they entered onto a beach. Turning to the north they dug their spurs into their horse's side and urged them into a gentle canter through the low waves. As the beach began to narrow and to avoid being caught by a turning tide they made their way inland up the cliffs and on reaching the top saw, in the distance the outline of a castle perched on a high spur of rock jutting out into the sea.

They made for it hoping to find some shelter and some hay for their horse's that is if anyone still lived there. The nearer they came to the castle they could see that it was not very large. The outer wall with a gateway and three towers were built precariously on the steep slopes of rock that were washed below by angrily looking waves crashing against them.

Crossing a wooden bridge that joined the rock to the mainland they passed through the open gateway and into a courtyard that was lined on one side with stables and on the other with what they took to be a row of servants' accommodation. Facing them directly opposite the gateway was the larger of the towers, a fortified building with a large solid iron studded wooden door. The strange thing was there was no one to be seen. Not a child, not a person, or an animal, no one. They made their way to what they correctly surmised were the stables and found hay and water in plentiful quantities so the horses were at last able to be fed and rested.

The lack of anyone about and the unnatural silence of the place left the pair feeling uneasy.

"What do you think?" asked Alan "where is everyone? There should be someone around."

"I don't know." Replied Daniel "But we should find someone in the main tower. Let's go and introduce ourselves."

Making their way across the cobbled courtyard they arrived at the door of the large tower. Several steep, narrow steps led up to the door making it difficult for anyone to try and force an entry. As they looked for a way to announce their presence the door swung silently inwards to reveal a dimly lit hallway. Hesitantly they stepped inside and as their eyes adjusted to the gloom they made out the figure of an elderly man wrapped in a long dark cloak standing facing them. The man was tall with a long grey beard and grey straggly hair protruding from beneath the leather skullcap that he wore. Before either of the two Cavaliers could speak the man stepped towards them.

"Welcome to Camelot." He said. "My name is Merkle," he added smilingly. "I am here as the watch keeper of this building and as messenger for the Ancients. I see that you have travelled far and must be very tired and hungry. Come follow me."

Not waiting for a reply or explanation from the pair he turned and led the way along a dimly lit passage.

"Did you hear what he called this place?" asked Alan turning to Daniel.

"I've heard of Camelot in stories my grandfather told me. Legend has it that it was the home of King Arthur and his Knights of the Round Table, you must have been told the same stories when you were little."

"Yes of course I have." Replied Daniel, "But surely this can't be the same place. Perhaps the old man is living a dream or has lost his mind a little."

They arrived in what they took to be a kitchen and on the table were two steaming bowls of pottage and two full pewters of Ale. Freshly baked bread was heaped on a plate in the centre of the table; its mouth-watering smell intensified the hunger felt in the bellies of the two men.

"Sit and enjoy the food." instructed Merkle. "We will talk later."

The two didn't need much encouragement and were soon enjoying the best meal they had ever tasted.
The tall man joined them at the table and sat silently watching them enjoy the food.

In between mouthfuls Daniel glanced over at the old man. "Are you here on your own then?" He asked enquiringly. Wondering how fresh hay was in the stables and how the hot food on the table had just been cooked.

"I am never alone." Merkle replied. "Just because you cannot see others does not mean that they are not there."

Daniel and Alan shared knowing glances at each other thinking that the old man was not quite right in the head.

It seemed as if Merkle read their minds. "Do not mock what you do not understand." He told them reproachfully.

"Sorry we did not intend to be disrespectful." replied Daniel, "You said this place was called Camelot, is this the same Camelot as the one in all of the tales that we have heard?" he asked enquiringly.

"I'm not sure of the tales that you have heard but there is only one Camelot as far as I know and this is it." He replied.

"So how long has Camelot been here?" Daniel asked

"Ever since the Ancients decided this is where it should be." Merkle answered.

"Who are the Ancients?" asked Alan.

"The Ancients were put here to oversee the world that we know and what takes place in it." answered Merkle.

"So who put the Ancients here? Where did they come from?"
"The power that created everything that you see brought them here."

"And what is this power?"

"The power of goodness of course. When a person is born and brought to this world they retain some of the goodness inside themselves. But just as surely as there is an opposite of most things there is also an opposite of goodness and that is badness.
There is an eternal battle between the two and it is the Ancients place to ensure that badness does not win. Badness has a way of creeping into us.
Sometimes badness does win and causes us to do things that we wouldn't normally do. I am sure that you must have often felt what you are doing is either right or wrong, good or bad." asked Merkle

The pair quietly agreed with what Merkle had asked.

"Is it possible to meet with the Ancients?" asked Daniel

"No, not in this world but perhaps in another." Merkle answered smiling.

"I don't understand." said Daniel.

"Do not concern yourself just accept that whatever path you take in your life and whatever you do it is meant to be."

Tilting his head to one side Merkle became quiet and appeared to be studying something and then suddenly he was no longer there with them he had disappeared before their eyes. Looking at each other in puzzlement at their host's disappearance but not wishing to leave any of the tasty food before them the two carried on eating and then just as sudden as Merkle had disappeared he reappeared.

"You have some friends following you I see?" he asked enquiringly while raising his eyebrows.

Alan and Daniel looked at each other with some alarm. The Roundheads must have caught up with them.

"I see that they are not friends of yours then. Come with me." He ordered.

He led the way up a spiral staircase set back in the wall that led up onto the battlements of the tower. He pointed along the beach to where a group of buff coated riders their steel breastplates and lobster-tail helmets glinting in the morning sun, could be seen heading towards them.

The troop of Roundheads must have split up into smaller units so that they could search in various directions. There were seven riders now approaching the bridge leading into the courtyard of the castle led by their commander, Captain Jeremiah Hopkins, a staunch Parliamentary supporter with an unpleasant reputation. Hopkins was a cruel man in his early thirties with a fearsome reputation of giving no quarter to any of the King's supporters. He had ordered the burning of villages suspected of harbouring any of the King's men seeking shelter and hanging those villagers that he had found guilty. His own men also feared him because of the harsh punishments he inflicted on any of them for what he considered to be the slightest infringement of military discipline. Standing at just short of six feet and with wide shoulders Jeremiah Hopkins was used to being obeyed without question.

Looking down at the Roundheads dismounting in the courtyard the two friends realized that there would be no way out in that direction. The only thing that they could do was to make a stand against the soldiers here in the Keep even though it might prove to be a 'one sided fight'.

Merkle read their thoughts. "There will be no fighting here. It is forbidden." If you flee they will catch up with you, your horses are still not refreshed, and if you hide they will search until they find you."

"What do you suggest we do then? Asked Daniel. "Fly away."

"There is a way." replied Merkle. "This castle of Camelot was once home to King Arthur and his knights and also the Wizard Merlin." He added with a faint smile.
"One day when the need is there they might all return, but perhaps in a different guise from what they are remembered as? We shall have to be patient and wait and see." His voice trailed off before it picked up again and he spoke in a louder voice.
"You were fortunate that you came across us today because the castle is not always visible only at certain times when the Celestial Coordinates and Magnetic Lines of Force are true. The Ley Lines of the Ancients are never stationary. They are always moving so it

is only when these meet up with the others to form a crossroads that the castle can be seen. It's obvious that you were meant to be here for some purpose. Perhaps we are about to find out what that purpose is."

They didn't understand a word of what he had said.

"You mentioned that there is a way." Alan broke in as he watched the Roundheads down below in the courtyard.

"Yes but it requires courage. Are you up for that?" He answered.

"We don't have much option." said Alan.

"Come then." Merkle instructed and led the way back down to the kitchen and then back along the passage to the hallway.

Moving to the rear of the hallway he drew back a curtain revealing a low wooden door. Opening the door Merkle stepped through followed by the two friends. Roughly hewn stone steps led down into the depths below the castle. As they progressed downwards torches would mysteriously burst into flame lightning their way. The steps ended in a passage that continued to slope downwards.

Moving along the passage they passed several doors and some iron barred cells until finally arriving at a larger door secured with several iron bolts. Merkle touched the door and the bolts slid back allowing the door to swing inwards into a large room that had been carved from the rock. In the centre of the room was a large bench covered with bottles and containers of various shapes and sizes. Along the walls were shelves filled with parchments and dust covered books. At the far wall was another curtain, which Merkle drew aside. It concealed an iron-studded oak door.

"Behind this door lies your means of evading those that seek you." He said. "But I cannot tell you where it leads as there are many paths. It is said that those that have entered have never returned. That is why I said that you must have courage to take this path."

"What say you Alan?" asked Daniel, "Are you for it or shall we surrender ourselves to the mercy of the Roundheads? Knowing what that will be."

"Let's do it." replied his friend. "Let's take the opportunity before us. It can't be worse than what otherwise awaits us."

They turned to Merkle. "Open the door Merkle. Let us pass through and with God's blessing all will be well."

"Very well then. I wish you both a safe journey wherever you go."

He opened the door. It was pitch black, not a sign of any light. "Take my hand Alan," Said Daniel 'and we'll both go through together."

Drawing their swords so as to be prepared against whatever they might encounter and grasping each other's hand they stepped into the darkness.

The Roundheads had dismounted and soon discovered the two horses in the stables along with the two damp cloaks. Captain Hopkins ordered the soldiers to split up into pairs to search different parts of the castle; he himself led two of the soldiers to the main tower to begin their search.

They were met by Merkle who greeted them as he had done with his two previous guests. Captain Hopkins demanded that he tell him where the two Cavaliers were hiding. When Merkle replied truthfully that he did not know where they were, Hopkins went to draw his sword to threaten Merkle with it. But no matter how he tried he could not draw the sword from its scabbard and neither could the two soldiers draw theirs.

"What devilry is this?" demanded Hopkins. "Seize him." He ordered the two soldiers.

Hurrying to obey the two men tried to take hold of Merkle but were prevented by some form of a force field surrounding the old man.

"Violence is not allowed here. I do not know where those that you seek are but I can show you where they have gone. It would be up to you if you decided to follow."

"Take us then quickly before they can escape." demanded Hopkins.

Merkle led them down the underground room and the curtained door. Drawing back the curtain he opened the door so that the three soldiers could see the blackness within.

"Be warned." He told them "Those that enter do so at their own peril for they may never return."

"Poppycock." replied Hopkins. "Get in there and search for the traitors." He ordered the two soldiers.

The two men held back clearly perturbed by the words from Merkle.

"Get in there I say." And grabbing the shoulder of both men he dragged them into the darkness.

The other soldiers had completed their search of the castle and were gathered in the courtyard awaiting further orders from their leader. Instead of their leader Merkle arrived and advised them that Captain Hopkins would not be returning and that they should leave the castle immediately.

"Be warned," he told them. "Do not linger here as the light falls or you may never leave at all."

The soldiers made to take hold of him, not used to being given orders by a civilian let alone an old man. But to their astonishment Merkle disappeared before them. They then tried to enter the tower to search for their commander but could not force the door. Heeding what the old man had said and with daylight beginning to fade they decided to retrace their steps and find the main party. They would return at a later date once they had received fresh orders.

As they left the castle Merkle, or was it Merlin, looked down on them from the high battlements and as they rode off along the beach a sea mist gradually engulfed the castle until it was totally lost from sight.

Part 2
Chapter 2

The Journey

As the two Cavaliers stepped through the door into the darkness they felt as if they were hurtling through space tumbling over and over amongst intermittent bright shards of light for what seemed to be an eternity but was in fact for only a short time. The tumbling stopped and they found themselves lying on their backs looking up at the sky.

What the two of them had experienced was passing through a Wormhole, a freak of nature that led from one timeline to another.

A ragged volley of muskets firing and a loud cheer from men startled them as they recognized the sharp smell of burning gunpowder as the blue haze of gun smoke drifted over them. The loud drumming of a horse's hoofs through the turf made them quickly sit up. Behind them were a line of Royalist troops busy reloading their muskets while to their front was a line of Parliamentary troops waving the fists in anger. Their first concern though was with the rider fast approaching them. The rider reigned in his horse bringing it to a sharp halt. They were relieved to find that it was one of the Royalist officers. They both rose to their feet, sheathing their swords, ready to greet the officer.

"What are you doing here?" he cried to them. "You're not supposed to be here, get back to your positions."

Looking past the two friends only a short distance down the field, the rider saw the three Roundheads as they rose slowly to their feet. He turned his horse and galloped towards them.
Hopkins was the first to regain his senses and spot the Royalist horseman bearing down on them. Leaping to his feet and drawing his sword he made to defend himself.

"You men are out of position. Get back to your line." Shouted the rider.

As he neared the Roundhead leader, Hopkins lunged with his sword at the rider piecing his thigh causing the rider to cry out in pain.

"What are you doing you idiot." The rider shouted.

Hopkins made to strike again but the rider pulled the horse away from the danger. Hopkins chased after the rider shouting obscenities and threating all kinds of violence but gave up as the distance between them widened. The rider galloped off to find a first aid station to stop the bleeding to his leg and report the incident.

Hopkins then spotted the two Cavaliers who stood motionless, witnessing the brief skirmish. Daniel locked eyes with Hopkins and seeing the madness in them called for Alan to run for the Royalist lines.

"After them." ordered Hopkins to his two companions, and with their swords held high they ran after the Cavaliers.
Wearing lighter calf length boots the Cavaliers were able to increase the distance from their pursuers who waddled along in their thigh length leather cavalry boots.

Heading for what they believed to be a scattering of low brightly covered huts the two friends were surprised to find the huts were supported on sets of low wheels of a strange, soft substance. Out of sight from their pursuers they rolled under one of the caravans taking cover in the shadows and lying still with baited breath, watching as the Roundheads went running past.

The rider who was the event controller arrived at the St Johns Ambulance First Aid Station where he had the wound to his leg stitched and dressed. He called for security to report the assault and request that the perpetrators be arrested.

Pictures relayed from a drone that was hovering above the battlefield soon gave the position of the three wanted men. The Police donned on their Jet Packs that enabled them to fly direct to any incident and soon had the three men cornered against a wooden farm building, where they called upon them to throw down their swords. The three Roundheads were totally confused at the sight of flying men and the circumstances that they found themselves in. They didn't know where they were or who these troops dressed in strange uniforms that they didn't recognize were, or why they were asking for their surrender.

"We are loyal Parliament soldiers on official business of Cromwell." They answered defiantly refusing to lay down their swords. The Police then with no other option fired their Tasers at the men allowing the three to be safely handcuffed and placed into custody.

Meanwhile the two Cavaliers not knowing that their pursuers were *hors-de- combat,* were trying to loose themselves amongst the many caravans and mobile homes that took up a corner of the large field.

A door of one of the caravans opened and a young slim girl in her early twenties dressed in faded jeans and a checked shirt stepped out.

"Hi there you two." She greeted them, "Who is it you're looking for?"

As they tried to conceal themselves behind a near caravan, she walked over to confront them.

"Can I help you?" she asked enquiringly. "I know most of the folk around here."

Worrying about being found by their pursuers, they decided to put their trust in the girl.

"The truth is," Daniel, replied, "there are some men after us who intend to deliver us some harm. Can you give us shelter until they have gone?"

After weighing up the pair and considering herself a good judge of character she decided that they could be trusted and indicated that they should enter her caravan.

After locking the door and closing all of the curtains she began to ask them for their story but before they could reply there was a loud knock on the door. Drawing their swords fearing that it was the Roundheads they stood ready to fight. The girl went to one of the windows and saw that it was her father being helped by one of the first aiders.

"It's my father," she reassured them and unlocking the door helped in a tall man in his mid-forties with dark brown hair.

The two friends immediately recognized the man as the rider on the horse that they had seen earlier in the field.
The girl thanked the first aider who left to return to their post. Supporting the twelve stone frame of her father the girl showed a hidden strength as she guided him to one of the soft chairs.

"What happened to you?" she asked pointing to his bandaged leg.

He explained saying that someone had become so carried away with their role as a Roundhead that they had attacked him. As he settled into a comfortable chair he pointed to the two friends, who had now sheathed their swords, and asked who they were.

"I was just about to find out." She answered.

26

Alan and Daniel introduced themselves and gave a long explanation from the time they had left Hexham to stepping through the Worm Hole in the castle to the attentive father and daughter.

Father and daughter held their questions but looked at each other with a mixture of amazement, puzzlement and disbelief. Until eventually when the two friends had finished their tale the girl's father addressed them both.

"Your story is quite amazing. There are many theories about time travel but so far none have been proven. It would really be worldwide news if this gets out. Of course your lives would never be the same and you'll probably be locked away in some government research establishment while they examine you. Not something to look forwards to. By the way my name's Mark McDade, and this," he said, indicating the girl, "if she hasn't already introduced herself, is my daughter Claire."

"I haven't had the chance." said Claire smiling at the two friends.

"I've never thought that I would meet someone from another time." stated the girl's father. "Do you think that you can find the entrance to this door if it exists or where it was that you found yourselves in the field where you arrived?"

"The door was in the castle if we could find the castle then yes we could find it. But with regards to the field, it is doubtful." answered Daniel.

"Just thought I would ask." said Mark. "Unfortunately there are no castles near here and we're some distance from the coast."

After a pause Mark looked at the two friends and asked "What year do you think it is?"

"Why it's 1645." replied Daniel.

"And who is head of the Royal family?" was Mark's second question.

"His Majesty King Charles I of course." answered Alan.

"Well for your information, the year is 2026 and King Charles III is the King of England. You have arrived at a re-enactment of the Battle of Naseby organized by the Sealed Knot Society at which King Charles I lost the Battle and was taken prisoner by Scottish troops who eventually passed him on to Parliament. I think a history lesson wouldn't go amiss. Claire teaches history at advanced level so if you speak nicely to her I'm sure she'll be only too pleased to help out."

"It's not just history that you require to know. There are many things you must learn about and that's going to take some time." said Claire. "The world is a totally different one from the one that you knew. It will take some time for I'm sure you'll have many questions to ask."

"I take it that you have nowhere to go." interrupted Mark. "So I think it best if you stay here for now. In any case security will still be looking for those characters that assaulted me and perhaps you two as well. We don't want them picking you up by mistake. We can sort other things out later. It's some coincidence that you hail from Hexham though because that's our home also. If you wish you'll be quite welcome to travel back there with us. " He finished off.

The two friends thought about what Mark had said about becoming known to everyone or being incarcerated in some government prison.

"We'd be most pleased to travel with you and thank you for your offer." They replied.

"Don't you think it's strange that we all come from the same place and meet up here?" Claire asked the three men. "It's as if it was all planned out. We just don't know what lies ahead of us do we?" She added, as she took out some blankets and pillows from a storage cupboard and began to make up two beds on the caravan's sofas.

The re-enactment finished the following day and as agreed Alan and Daniel would travel back to Hexham with Mark and Claire. Father and daughter had discussed surrendering the two to the authorities but decided against it, as it would probably mean they would be treated as mentally deranged or concealed from the rest of the world until they had been drained of facts and then who knows what would happen. At least this way they could build a life for themselves and retain their freedom. Besides they quite liked the two young men.

To avoid being arrested by the Police if they were still being hunted, the pair were to be concealed in the false bottom of Mark's horsebox.

The horsebox had been specially constructed to be used at times in other activities that Mark was involved with.

"Just as long as the horse decides to hold its bladder." smiled Alan. "We should manage to survive."
"Don't worry," replied Mark smiling, "it has a waterproof membrane covering the floor."

Once well clear of the area and any Police road checks, Mark halted his LandRover and the horsebox at the first lay-by and released the two men from their cramped positions. Leaving their swords in the concealed compartment of the horse box they then transferred to the car that Claire was driving that was towing the caravan, as it was much more comfortable to travel in.

They travelled north along the A1 Motorway at a restricted speed of sixty miles an hour, a speed that the two friends had never experienced before. At first they were alarmed at the scenery flashing by but after a while they quite enjoyed the experience and enquired if they could go any faster.
The journey north was an eye opener for the two friends. They saw many things that left them with question after question, and how was it the metal box in which they travelled was driven by

something called electricity and without any horses to pull them or anyone to guide it except something called a 'Sat-Nav'.

The journey north took over them over five hours and was partly due to the halts at the number of check points maned by the Police and soldiers. Claire informed them these check points were because of the riots after the UK left the European Community to prevent illegal shipments of food by smugglers and black market racketeers.

Chapter 3

Hexham

The car guided by its own 'Sat-Nav' made an uneventful journey and before long they arrived in Hexham at Mark's house.

It was a large detached house on the outskirts of the town with several bedrooms. Along one side and set back from the house was a large outbuilding that included a fully fitted gym and a workshop where Mark maintained his collection of various bicycles. Mark's hobby was cycling. He enjoyed nothing more than the thrill of pedalling around the local country lanes at high speed, feeling the wind in his face as he sped along. It also helped him stay in peak condition a requirement demanded of his real profession as a Government employee.

They were greeted by Mark's wife Kathleen, an attractive slim brunette in her late-thirties but who looked like she had just turned twenty.

Kathleen was used to sudden arrivals in connection with her husband's business and after hearing their remarkable story had welcomed them both and helped them settle into their new accommodation.

Claire's younger sister Maureen also welcomed the two young males into what had previously been mainly a female dominated environment. Claire's two friends Lorna and Emma who had been lodging at the house had now left and lived nearby in the town with their partners.

It had been decided that Alan and Daniel could stay at Mark's house until they became more settled. The immediate priority was to find appropriate clothing for them both; none of Mark's were of a correct size. With some hesitation Mark surrendered his Bank Card to Maureen with instructions to go and buy clothes for them but knowing what a temptation some of the Girls Fashion shops in the town could be she was to make sure she returned with all of the receipts. Claire also insisted that before Daniel or Alan were allowed out of the house that they must have their long hair cut and shave off their moustaches and beards that were fashionable in King Charles I time but not quite in today's style.

Mark ran a small business manufacturing period style clothes and replica arms for the re-enactment societies. The business had originally been manufacturing clothing, shoes and leather crafts way back in time and for as long as anyone could remember. Now they were in the business of supplying bespoke clothing and accessories for enthusiasts, which were very much sought after. In discussion about the pair's immediate future it seemed appropriate that Daniel and Alan could be employed in the business adding their knowledge and skills from their time in the past to the business of today. He introduced the two friends to the workforce as distant cousins of his from the south of England which helped explain their accent and way of talking.

For the first few months the pair spent much of their time exploring this new Hexham that they found themselves in. They had at first looked for their homes and the forge but they had gone and instead rows of houses stood in their place. All that remained of what they knew was the Cathedral and the Old Gaol house and some of the narrow streets.

The first year quickly passed. Claire had given intensive history lessons to the pair. They were dismayed to learn that their King had been executed but pleased that his son Charles II had eventually taken his place as Monarch. The horrors of the two world wars and other successive conflicts and the numbers that lost their lives along with the means of destruction appalled them. What they found most incredulous though was that someone had been to the Moon and had returned back to earth.

Claire also found herself answering countless questions on a variety of subjects that the pair of newcomers knew nothing about along with the basics of everyday living. Monetary values, shopping and goods, electricity and gas supplies, radio and television, telephones, buses, trains, hygiene, the list went on but slowly they learned. Elocution lessons were also high on the agenda as they learned the modern way of speech.

Mark also contributed his share by introducing them to modern day firearms and accompanying them hunting in the surrounding woods where they quickly adapted to rifles and shotguns much to the decline of the rabbit population.

But what interested them most is how the country had arrived at the present situation. Claire had told them of BREXIT and the disastrous decision in 2020 to leave the European Union and the resulting chaos and turmoil it had caused.

 In the first three years of leaving the EU thousands of people had lost their jobs, trade agreements had not visualized, food and fuel had become short and many things that had been promised by the government or those that had driven BREXIT had just not happened.

The result was the people took to the streets demanding that the government put things right. There was mob rule with organized gangs roaming the streets looting and burning as they pleased. Law and order broke down with no one answerable for issuing orders to the Police. The Prime Minister had resigned leaving a weak government without anyone capable of taking the helm. It was the same with the opposition; no one wanted the *'poison chalice'* of being Prime Minister.

The Scottish Government and the Welsh Assembly had done their best to govern their own areas but without the support of Westminster they too soon collapsed.

The situation gradually worsened until finally the Queen took command of the situation. No longer prepared to watch her country break down into what was becoming a lawless free for all mess, she made her decision. The Queen summoned the Chief of the Defence Staff along with all members of the Defence Council including the First Sea lord, the Chief of the General Staff, Chief of the Air staff and the Commander of Joint Forces Command to a meeting. As the armed forces were the only functioning, disciplined force of order that remained in the country she reminded them of their 'Oath of Allegiance' to support her.

The Queen laid out before them her plans to save the country and declared a national emergency.

With the assistance of the armed forces the Queen brought some order to the country. Marshall Law was declared. The army was deployed on the streets while the other services manned radio and television buildings, power stations, reservoirs and water services, ports and airports and food distribution points. A curfew was imposed on the population and anyone taking part in a riot was likely to be shot.

The Queen dismissed parliament; those MPs that were held responsible for the mess were imprisoned although some had already met their fate at the hands of the mob and at the end of a rope. All political parties were made unlawful and membership carried a jail sentence.

It took two more years before some semblance of normality was restored to the country although much still remains to be done. More recently the Queen had decided to step down and had passed the Crown to her son Charles who is the present King Charles III. So once again the country was ruled by a monarchy. This of course is unacceptable to the many Republicans and those who have no love for the Royal's and wish to change things. So the threat to the King is always there.

The King with advice from his supporters agreed to the formation of a new political party called the Peoples Party that is now in Parliament and does make some decisions but only with agreement from the King. An opposition party is at present being considered but a decision on its formation has still yet to be made.

As well as practical advice and history lessons Claire took upon herself to show them how to behave in this new world they found themselves in and explain the wonders of what they saw. To help them with this she began taking them on day trips around the Region so they could see things close up.

Catching the train from Hexham into Newcastle Central Station was their first introduction to public transport from where they boarded the Metro to Newcastle Airport for a closer view of the airplanes that they had seen fly high overhead. They watched through the windows of the Terminal as lines of passengers climbed aboard the aircraft and the doors closed behind them. As the noise from the engines penetrated into the Terminal the two friends looked at Claire in alarm. She reassured them that all was well and went on to explain that this was the fastest and safest way for people to travel.

"The world is a lot smaller now than it was in your time." she told them "Not in size but in the time it would take you to travel to the other side of the world is what I mean. In your time it would take you nearly a year to sail to Australia where as in an aircraft it would only take you fifteen hours."

"Where is Australia?" asked Alan "I haven't heard of that place."

"It's on the other side of the world," Claire told him smiling, "I think geography lessons are needed as well."

They boarded the Metro back to Newcastle where Claire led them past the Castle Keep down the well-worn steps to the Quayside. While much of the area had been redeveloped she thought some places might be familiar to them. They marvelled at the strange shaped buildings on the other side of the river and at the bridges so high above them carrying trains and traffic across from both sides.

They were disappointed at the Quayside. It bore no resemblance to the one they remembered apart from one of the buildings that looked familiar. The ships and seamen and girls had all gone and the Taverns where they had spent so much time in visiting were no longer there.

"We had some good times here Alan." Said Daniel to his friend

"It's a shame it's all changed. Do you remember…?"

Claire interrupted their reminiscing stating, "I bet you two got up to no good here."

They all laughed together as they made their way back to the city centre.

It was a Saturday afternoon and the city was packed with shoppers and the crowds from the football game that had just finished.

"So many people," said Daniel "where do they all come from?"

"If you don't know now you never will." Claire replied laughing, "Where do you think?"

Daniel blushed "I didn't mean that." Daniel answered becoming stuck for words.

"I know what you mean." Claire replied, "It's becoming a problem worldwide. Populations are growing at an alarming rate. This puts a strain on the ecological system of the world on which we depend. It's only recently that the world has sat up and began to take note.

If we don't act quickly there will be no planet for our children and grandchildren to enjoy as we have."

Claire began to mention how the world was heating up due to man-induced climate change and how it was now being tackled by the world powers but as the questions began she decided to save that topic for later. Over the coming months she took the pair on several more excursions of which they all enjoyed.

During this time Claire and Daniel had become quite happy in each other's company and sought each other out whenever the occasion permitted. Claire had taught Daniel how to cycle although it had taken some time and several falls before he had finally mastered riding a bicycle. Daniel did admit though that he preferred a horse under him than these mechanical replacements.

They spent many hours on bikes borrowed from Marks collection, cycling around the local area exploring scenic places that Claire had known about from her childhood. While Daniel recognized some from his past, the modern infrastructure of buildings, bridges and roadway flyovers had replaced others that he had known.

One summer afternoon in a secluded wooded grove on the banks of the River Tyne they were enjoying a picnic that Claire had prepared. Claire asked Daniel about his previous life because he had never really talked about it.

"What would you like to know?" Daniel asked smiling.

"Tell me about your family? She replied. 'Do you have a wife or a partner where you came from?"

"I came from here remember, but in a different time." He replied smiling.

Daniel believed in honesty so looking Claire in the eye replied, "Yes I am or was married and my wife is called Denise and we have a young daughter Elizabeth.

They lapsed into silence for a while then Claire asked, "Would you go back if you could? You must miss them a lot." She added.

"That's a difficult question that you've asked." replied Daniel, "Of course I miss them both. I haven't seen or heard from them for the last three years while I was away serving the King, so I don't know if they are alive or not. Now I'll never know what they are doing or what became of them. It is strange being here today and thinking that my family lived and died over three hundred years ago and that there may well be descendants that I pass in the street that I don't even know of. "

"What we should do is to trace your family history as far back as we can. I have a friend at the school who is interested in Genealogy. I'll ask him if he'll do a search for us. We should have done this a while ago." Claire added.

After a short pause Daniel continued, "I don't think I would want to return to the time that I knew because while I would not want to desert my wife and daughter it would mean I would have to leave here and I wouldn't see you again, and I think that you know how my feelings are for you."

They were both quiet for a while until Claire looking at Daniel, said
"It's no good living in the past with your memories you must live for today and make the most of the life that you have left. Life is too short not to enjoy it."

Daniel knew what she said made sense and taking her hand in his asked her, "If you share the same feelings for me that I have for you, could there be a future for us both together. Please say yes?" he quietly added.

Claire looked into his eyes and kept him waiting before replying with a smile on her face. "I'm sure that there will be." as she kissed him on the cheek.

Daniel took her in his arms and as they held each other close the sweet smell of her hair filled his nostrils and he felt the soft contours of her body against his. They held each other close enjoying the warmth and comfort of each other until the sun began to fade and it was time for them to return home.

Over the coming months Mark and Kath could see that Claire and Daniel's friendship had developed into a deep relationship that would probably end in a marriage.
Claire and Daniel had discussed marriage but decided against it at this time. They both felt uncomfortable that Daniel had a wife already even though she was in a different time and decided to let things go as they were for the time being.

It was October of the second year of their arrival that Claire and Daniel, with the help of Mark paying the deposit, moved into a small two bedroomed flat near the centre of town. It was convenient for Daniel getting to the business premises and for Claire for catching the train to Newcastle where she now lectured at the University. It was soon after they moved into their flat that she discovered she was pregnant with Daniel's baby.

Alan still lived with Mark and Kath and had become very close with Maureen, Claire's younger sister, and had been for some months.

Chapter 4

Leicester

Captain Jeremiah Hopkins and his two companions Benjamin Castle and Nathan Levin had maintained their role as members of Oliver Cromwell's model army and without any other means of proving their identity had been held in Rampton Secure Hospital for violent prisoners while enquires were made to establish who they actually were.

They were being held under the 1983 Mental Health Act as men with a 'Dangerous and Severe Personality Disorder' who were considered a grave and immediate danger to the public after being detained running amuck dressed as they were, brandishing swords and stabbing a member of the public, namely, Mark.

Time passed more slowly for the trio, which gave them time to learn about this strange new world that they found themselves in. They were often asked if they were country boys because of the way that they pronounced certain words and after listening to their fellow inmates they soon learned to drop 'thee' and 'thou' from their vocabulary.

They slowly adjusted themselves pleading loss of memory to any searching questions realizing that the only way to become free men again was to go along with whatever their captors wanted to hear.

After two years the consultants at the hospital no longer considered them a danger to the public and they were released under the care of a probation officer and provided with a new National Insurance Number, Identity Card and temporary accommodation in Leicester. Prior to their release they had been asked where they wanted to relocate to. Hopkins remembered that Leicester had been a Parliamentary stronghold during the Civil War and decided that the three of them would locate there; after all they were still his soldiers and would follow his orders.

At about then same time that Hopkins and his companions had been detained at the Naseby re-enactment a chance meeting of two characters provided the foundation for what was to become a threat to the stabilization of the UK along with the involvement of the three Parliamentarians.

Richard Fox or 'Richie' as he was commonly known had a deep hatred for authority and anything connected to it including the Royal Family. He had while serving time in prison on several charges including larceny, and aggregated bodily harm become obsessed with putting his thoughts into action. He was determined to free the UK from the influence of what he considered the unnecessary deadweight of a Royal Family ruling the country.

He believed that the UK would be better off run as a Federal State and was actively seeking to implement his ideas by any means possible. He had a small but not insignificant band of followers on the outside of prison that were actively involved in carrying out his plans to influence a change in the way that the UK was run.

It was while in Leicester prison that he had become acquainted with James Radcliffe or Jimmy, as he was better known. Radcliffe was in jail for contempt of court and was the leader of a breakaway faction of the United Defence League, an outlawed Neo Nazi organization. While sharing the same cell Richie and Jimmy discussed and agreed on a plan uniting both of their organizations' into one, to become known as the Republic of Great Britain or RGB.

Because of Jimmy's connections with an outlawed organization a listening device had been inserted in their cell. All of their conversations were recorded and passed to the Security Services for examination. It was decided by them that this was just the rambling of two prisoners with wishful thinking; however a mark was placed against their files for future checks.

Richie became well known to the prison population after beating one of the prison's 'Queens' half to death after he had tried to molest him while in the showers. It was a few days later that three friends of the beaten man came to Richie's cell to even up the score and dish out their form of revenge. While Ritchie was a big man standing just over six feet Jimmy was of slighter build, but years of labouring on building sites had toned his body into hardened muscle and given him the strength of two men. Ritchie and Jimmy stood together against the avenging trio and sent them away in a worse state then when they had arrived. This incident cemented the friendship between the pair and let it be known that they stood for each other. No one bothered them again.

Jimmy was first to be released after serving a shorter sentence and was there to meet Ritchie when his sentence came to an end. They wasted no time in putting the plans they had discussed into practice. High on the list was recruitment and before long groups of trusted followers were established in towns and cities all over the country.

Over the following years as the RGB organization grew in size so also did its security problems with several of its members being arrested and placed in jail. Reorganization was carried out to form it into small separate Cells with only one person from each Cell

Group attending any of the larger Area Group Controller's meetings.

Only the Area Controller's in turn would attend a 'Select Meeting' called by Ritchie and Jimmy. The Area Controller's would bring with them a token amount of the monies acquired by their own area groups, enough to maintain the immediate funds of the central group; the remainder was 'laundered' by their own area organisation and a record of transactions given to the groups treasurer. This precaution avoided any electronic footprint between themselves and the RGB leaders.

The RGB had become 'The Group" in the UK, gradually wiping out and absorbing the smaller gangs that had previously held the monopoly in drugs, people trafficking, prostitution and protection rackets. When coming up against a problem gang usually in the big cities the RGB had formed an alliance with them in order to prevent a 'turf war' but provided an influence on their activities. Without any doubt Organisational Crime in the UK was being run by the RGB.

Their activities had attracted the attention of the National Crime Agency who had tried so far to penetrate the wall of silence that surrounded the group. Informers had be known to disappear before their torn and mangled bodies were left to be found as a warning to others tempted to provide information to the authorities.

The RGB 'Select Meeting' place was in the White Bull in an upstairs room away from any prying eyes. It was hired the first Friday of each month under the guise of a meeting by the RAOB and paid for in cash that suited the landlord just fine. Only bona-fide known members known to Ritchie or Jimmy were invited to attend which made it impossible for any outsiders to gate crash a meeting.

The Agenda rarely changed, the Area Controllers would deposit their monies with the RGB Treasurer, a National Bank employee, who would mark details into a Laptop computer and keep a regular record of each areas contribution. The actual monies were stowed into a backpack that he would take with him after the meeting and then be 'laundered' through his various connections. The Agenda would continue with each areas report; then any briefings by Ritchie or Jimmy and then a few beers before the meeting ended.

On their arrival in Leicester the three Parliamentarians were lodged into a hostel run by a prisoners release programme.
The Hostel was located in a row of pre-war terraced flats, three of which had been converted into one joined up house of twelve

bedrooms. The residents were expected to share bedrooms with others who had recently been released and depending on the number living there it could become crowded.

On arrival the three Roundheads were allocated to one room on their own on the upstairs floor at the front of the building that suited them fine.

They received a small weekly allowance that was adequate for them to buy necessities until they found work. As well as attending the Local Job Centre where they registered for work they also had to report weekly to a liaison officer on their progress.

The confines of one bedroom for the three of them and the Spartan facilities of the Hostel were not conducive to relaxation. Seeking more comfortable surroundings they began visiting the nearest Public House which was the White Bull.

It was here while frequenting the White Bull, that the three Roundheads became established with the group who were known as the RGB.

At first the regulars in the Pub had greeted the three with suspicion but after a while they accepted their presence as some their own kind. One evening a regular who was a member of RGB encouraged them to talk about themselves. They were careful about what they said and only repeated on what they had agreed upon about recently being discharged from hospital.

Their views on what they thought about the King and the Royal family crept into the conversation. On discovering that they were not supporters of the Royals but instead staunch Republicans, the regular suggested that they might be able to earn a few extra pounds if they became members of the RGB to which they readily agreed.

Chapter 5

The White Bull

During the last few months there had been a spate of burglaries in and around the surrounding areas of Leicester.

The White Bull Inn is one of Leicester's less salubrious pubs and is well known as a gathering point for characters that had no respect for the law. It had a well-known reputation of being a likely place where stolen goods were exchanged for drugs or money although the Police had no conclusive proof of this. However due to the increase in burglaries and because of the Police's suspicions it had been decided to place twenty-four hour surveillance on the premises.

During the weekly maintenance of street lights two men dressed as workmen had installed a concealed camera in one of the streetlights directly opposite the main door of the pub. This provided a continuous stream of photographs of those entering and of those leaving to the Police headquarters where a team of detectives could look through the photos for known suspects and record the dates when they visited.

It was also noted that known troublemakers from other towns made regular visits on the first Friday of each month. A separate database file of these was opened and the data added to the Police National Database.

Real time comparisons of the Police National Database against the Security Services Database searched for any known or suspected dissidents on their 'radar'. Artificial Intelligence Facial Recognition software picked up images of both Ritchie and Jimmy as regular visitors to the White Bull on the days that meetings were held. As both of them had a flag on their files a closer scrutiny of the recorded tapes taken while they were in prison revealed that RGB was mentioned many times.

It was not known at this time that the White Bull was the meeting place of the 'Heads' of the RGB and that it was from here that an illegal National Organization was being controlled.

Mark had been called to London for a meeting. He told the family it was for something to do with the family business and he might be away for a few days.

Mark's business trip took him to Thames House, Milbank adjacent to Lambeth Bridge, which is the headquarters of MI5 Britain's Security Service.

Mark had been a member of the Security Service for several years; his activities with the Sealed Knot Society provided him with ideal cover and ample opportunity to participate in any on-going security operations.

The Security Services had discovered that something big was being planned that would split the country in two just as it had been during the BREXIT fiasco. Details were scarce but it was known that the group calling themselves RGB was involved. It was just one of many that came to their attention but this one involved a group of Neo Nazis and disenchanted Republicans who had a large following in all of the major towns and cities of the UK. One of the MI5 operatives had managed to infiltrate the group and was sending back reports that alarmed the senior MI5 management. The report named 'The White Bull' as being a meeting point for the 'higher ups' of the group but more information was required.

The meeting at Thames House had been called because of these reports and to formulate a plan of action for monitoring the RGB.

Mark entered Thames House by a discreet side door and after going through security checks was escorted to a third floor briefing room. Several other members of the Service were seated around a large table some of whom Mark recognized having worked with them on previous occasions. When it was obvious that all of those summoned were in attendance, the door at the far end of the room opened and the Operations Controller and his assistant entered.

Taking his seat the Controller greeted the gathered Operators. "Good morning everyone, nice to see you all again. I've asked you all here today because of information that we have received about a group calling themselves the RGB. Our friends in the National Crime Agency have had this group on their radar for some time now but have not been able to get anyone inside it. They have asked if we can help out and of course," he added with a smile, "I said that we would be delighted. We understand this group are planning something big but we don't at the moment know exactly what it is or when it will occur. We have to learn more about this RGB group and what is going on at the meetings they have at this Pub in Leicester." stated the MI5 Controller.

He pressed one of the buttons on the desk in front of him and images of the White Bull appeared on a large screen set high up on the wall. He pressed the button again to display fresh images. "We already know that these two characters," he pointed to the photos of Radcliffe and Fox, "are involved and of the identity of some of these others. There is one that we can't identify, mainly because he always has his baseball cap pulled low and we can't get a good photo of him. He always leaves the meeting carrying a heavy satchel and is escorted by a couple of heavies and then they all drive off somewhere. What's he got in that bag and where does he go? "Peter," he turned to his assistant, "I want the Midlands Team to find out ASAP what these people are up to."

He next turned to Mark, "Mark I want you to go with the Midlands Team and provide them with support and advice. You haven't been in that area before so you should be clear to operate around there. I'm relying on you to get the answers that I want"

There was more business to discuss concerning the other Operators and their areas of interest until the meeting finally closed.

The Midlands Team was contacted and told to expect Mark who would brief them on what had been discussed and instructions to stand by for an important operation.

The Security Services have strategically placed centres throughout the UK where their Operators can call upon for support or use as safe places to rest or hold someone for a short time. These centres might front as a garage or a warehouse or some other bona fide business. They are equipped to provide the Operators with whatever equipment or transport they might require or the means of providing it.

Mark caught the train to Manchester where outside of the station he was met by one of the Operators from the Midlands Team. Catching a tram across the city they left it at the stop nearest to the Midlands MI5 Support Centre and walked the remainder of the way.

The Support Centre had in its previous existence been a Garage selling and repairing cars and vans. The owner had unfortunately lost a lot of money due to his gambling habit and was forced to sell the business to pay his debts.

The new owners, the Security Services, had advertised the new business as a Storage Management Repository and had stocked the floor of what had been the workshop with empty shipping containers and large crates. Whenever the office was approached with requests from potential customers they were informed that unfortunately the storage was fully booked but they could try again at a later date.

After meeting with the others of the team Mark briefed them on what the Operations Controller had told him. Arrangements were then made to visit Leicester Police Headquarters where they requested all of the information available on the White Bull.

Every Friday morning the Landlord of the White Bull made a weekly visit to the Cash and Carry warehouse that was on the outskirts of Leicester. There he would load up his old van with bottles of spirits and sundries that he would sell in addition to those supplied by the Brewery. It was one way of supplementing the meagre wage he received for managing the pub.

It was not very long after the Landlord had left on his weekly trip that a blue van from the local electricity services drew to a halt in the street alongside of the pub and two men dressed in overalls got out.

They walked across the road and knocked on the front door. It was answered by the Landlords wife still wrapped in her dressing gown and with curlers still in her hair.

"Yes what is it?" she asked impatiently.

"Morning Missus," replied the taller of the men, as he showed her his ID card.

"We're from the Electricity Board. Can we speak to the person who pays the Electric Bill please? Or would that be you?" he asked knowing that it was not.

She gave a fleeting glance at the ID card as she replied that it was her husband that they should speak to but that he's not here just now but would be back later if they would like to come back then.

"That's a pity." said the tall man. "We've called because we understand that you are being charged for more electricity then what you actually use. Do you have a smart meter?" He asked. He could see her thinking.

"Eh yes I think so." She answered.

"Yes we thought so it probably needs checking over. It seems to be producing a surge in the readings now and then. Well unfortunately we have a busy schedule and won't be able to call back until next month so you'll continue to be overcharged until we can check the system." and turning he and his friend made to leave.
"Wait a minute." She cried. "As you're here you might as well do your checks."

She held open the door for them to enter. If her husband found out that she had sent them away and he found out that it would be costing them money, there would be an awful row.

"It won't take us long. We'll be in and out before you can say 'Bob's your uncle,' Show us where the meter is love. A nice cup of tea would be very welcome. Milk no sugar please." he added.

She led them along a passage and pointing to a cupboard told them she thought the meter was in there. She left them to go and put the kettle on.
They opened up the cupboard and plugged in a hand held monitor to an USB port. The woman returned with two cups of tea.

"Something's wrong here." said one of the men. "Look at the meter. It should show a steady indicator, but when I press this button we get a higher reading. It's not the smart meter's fault though that seems OK. I think the fault could be in the wiring. I think it best if we check out the rooms while we are here. How many rooms do you have love?" He asked.

It was agreed that there was four downstairs rooms including the bar, snug, lounge and kitchen and three rooms upstairs, two bedrooms and the meeting room come storage room.

"Let's start upstairs and work our way down to the bar. That way we should find the problem more quickly."

They started in the bedrooms opening up the plug sockets to check that they worked and tested the room lights and switches until the Landlords wife became bored watching them and went downstairs to watch the TV. Finding the meeting room locked they called down for the woman to bring up the room key. Muttering to herself that she had things to do and could do without all this hassle she opened up the room and then returned to her television program. Entering the meeting room they found inside several stacks of chairs, cardboard boxes and rolled up spare carpets heaped around the walls. While in the centre of the room was a large table surrounded by several chairs.

While one of the men closed the room door and placed some chairs behind it so that it couldn't be opened without the chairs falling over the other man unlocked their toolbox and removed the inner false lid and drew out the latest innovation in eavesdropping technology.

These were imitation spiders that by means of a miniature camera equipped with a powerful amplifier could send verbal and visual transmissions at the same time. A lifelong battery that was recharged by any light source powered them. They could also move on a vertical surface the same as a real spider. This was made possible by a special adhesive on each of its legs that could be switched on and off by electrical pulses. Once established in situ the spider could be positioned to best advantage either by its operator or by the sound of the nearest human voice.

The men positioned a spider high on the wall at each end of the room and removing the mobile transmitter from the toolbox clicked it once to indicate to Mark who was sat in a Ford Transit Van at the end of the street, that mission was accomplished. They waited to hear the pre-arranged two clicks to indicate that vision and sound was being received satisfactory.

As soon as they received the clicks they went downstairs locking the door behind them and returned the key to the woman informing her that they had found and fixed the fault in the wiring so there was no further work required and that she wouldn't be charged for their work so no need to worry about extra electricity charges.

That evening a group of 'bikers' loitering at the end of the street had, by the look of things, a problem as one of them on his knees was tinkering with the engine of one of the motorbikes. The four men dressed, as "Hell's Angels" were a rough looking bunch and of the type to steer well clear of.

From information provided by the Police Mark and the team began making preparations for the forth coming operation. Having been informed that the RGB meetings took place on the first Friday of the month they made sure that they would be ready for the task ahead.

Earlier that day Mark and his colleagues had visited the Manchester Security Services Centre where they collected two Harley Davison Motorbikes. Mark took one of them for a trial run but couldn't adapt to the cow-horn type handlebars and returning to the centre requested the mechanics to fit the bike with more conventional handlebars that were more to his likening. The next step was to look the part.

The Centre had a well-stocked room full of clothing of all styles for all occasions. They dressed themselves as 'Hell's Angels' and had much fun choosing stick on facial hair and stick-on tattoos. With longhaired wigs that protruded from under their German army style helmets they certainly looked the part. Satisfied with their preparations they had a meal and a final briefing before leaving for the long ride to Leicester and taking up position near to the White Bull.

The group of 'Hell's Angels" waited patiently, ready to follow the wearer of the baseball cap when he left the White Bull. While pretending to repair a problem with one of their motorbikes they had listened in to the transmissions made by the surveillance spiders from inside the White Bull's meeting room and were ready to go when the meeting finished.

At nine thirty their target and the heavies left the pub and climbed into the car that drew up at the entrance. As the car containing the three men pulled away Mark pressed the starter button on his motor bike and with a second Operator on his pillion followed the car at a reasonable distance. The other bike soon caught up with them and took turns at being the nearest to the car.

Eventually as they reached the other side of the city the car pulled up at a row of terraced houses fronted by small gardens in a quiet street lit only with two streetlights. The car drew to a stop and their target carrying his satchel got out and entered into one of the houses. Seeing their passenger safely home the car accelerated away leaving the street quiet once again. The Operator on Mark's pillion dismounted and leaving his crash helmet with Mark casually walked past the house noting the street's name and the target's house number. Returning to Mark he climbed back on the pillion and they made off for the Police Station. As the "Hell's Angels" entered the Police Station they were viewed with suspicion by the Desk Sergeant until after presenting their Identity Cards to the Senior Duty Superintendent they were accepted through the security gate into the rear offices.

Requesting coffee and a computer that he could use Mark loaded a copy of the Electoral Role onto the screen and soon discovered the identity of the man in the Baseball cap. The man at 5b Crowcroft Road was listed as Ian Blacklock who lived there with his wife Irene Blacklock. No children were listed. Checks on the Police National Database showed that he had no criminal record. Further checks with HMRC showed that he was employed by 'The Associated Bank of Northern Trustees'. His wife Irene was employed by the NHS as an Admin Clerk at the local hospital.

The house at Number 5b was then put under surveillance so that more could be learned about its occupants, their comings and goings and what visitors they had. The team soon had a detailed dossier of the house and were surprised at the number of visitors that it had.

It was decided that entry to the house was required without the occupants' knowledge.

Additional members would be required for this operation to ensure everything went smoothly. Entry would take place mid-morning after Blacklock and his wife had gone to work. On the morning of the planned entry an operator took up position at either end of the street. Their job would be to delay Blacklock or his wife if they returned while the team were in the house.

A white Van displaying 'Superior Pest Control' along its sides pulled up outside of the house and out got Mark and his two colleagues dressed in white overalls. If they were asked who they were they would say that they had been called in because of a Rat infestation, which usually kept people clear of the area.

Carrying toolboxes and some other larger items they made to the front door and after ensuring that no one was at home and they were not being observed two of them quickly placed the larger item, which was a hydraulic jack across the door with its legs against each side of the doorframe. After a few pumps of the handle the doorframes bent slightly just enough for the lock to become free of its constraint and the door opened inwards. Releasing the jack the three men stepped inside and locked the door's deadbolt behind them.

One of the men went quickly to the back door and made sure it was unlocked. This would be the quick way out if needed. They began a pre-arranged methodical search of the two bedroomed flat looking for the satchel while one of them placed listening devices in the main rooms. The satchel was soon discovered in the bottom of a cupboard covered by an old blanket. Before disturbing it Mark took a quick photo of it with his mobile phone. Opening the satchel they discovered bundles of currency each of different denomination but the majority of which were of twenty pound notes.

Along with the banknotes were several passports each by a different name although they were all for the same person identified by the photograph. These were also photographed.

Of more interest though was what they had come for the laptop computer. Mark switched it on only to find it was password protected. No matter, he placed a memory stick into one of the USB slots and booted the computer up again. The memory stick contained a software program developed by GCHQ that would bypass the password protection and any security software on the laptop. Mark soon had access to the 'innards' and began copying all of the documents to the memory stick.

As soon as the copying was complete Mark logged into a web-site run by GCHQ and began downloading another program onto the laptop. This was modified BIOS that would allow the Security Services to remotely access the laptop at any time without the knowledge of its owner. Once complete everything was put back as it was, the satchel covered exactly as it had been with the old blanket, the back door relocked and the trio left the house.

Back at the Police Station Mark loaded the documents from the memory stick onto his laptop. On opening one of the Spread Sheets it gave a list of monthly monies collected at the RGB meetings. It also contained the names of the visiting Area Controllers and how much they gave each month and from which area they came. Unfortunately it only gave the first name or nickname and no surnames. That would make the job of tracing them a bit harder but not impossible.

Other Spread Sheets listed local names of 'Money Mules' and a record of their transactions in what was believed to be a money laundering operation. Visitors to the house would collect monies and pay it into their own bank accounts and then either transfer it to an account controlled by Blacklock or on to another mule as directed. He had set up several companies that made it look as if they supplied the mules with goods that made the companies appear as genuine. He would as one of the businesses supply the mule with a receipt for the goods they supposedly purchased. The mules would then receive a small payment for this service.

Mark wasted no time in informing MI5s Controller on what he had discovered; disappointingly there was nothing to give any ideas as to what RGB was planning.

The Controller gave permission to share the names from the Spread Sheet along with photographs of those that attended the meeting to all of the mentioned areas Police forces. Special attention should be given to those with any connection to James Radcliffe, Richard Fox or any a group called the RGB. With a comprehensive investigation they may be able to identify the men and notify MI5 in order that surveillance teams could be put in place. Details of the money laundering however were to be kept away from the Police for the time being. The Controller didn't want a Police operation taking place and giving the game away about how they had obtained the information and compromising the on-going operation.

Chapter 6

The King

King Charles had been the longest-serving heir to the crown in British History, now his long awaited wish had come true and he was now King of England.

Charles was an ecologist. He had over the years supported many projects in many parts of the world. He had founded a number of initiatives both locally and globally including fisheries and rain forest conservation. He was a strong supporter of those actively striving to reduce climate change by cleaning the air and bringing down air pollution.

Now that he was King and in the present situation that the UK was in, Charles was in a better position to introduce his ideas to the British Isles. Now with complete authoritarian power Charles issued some Royal Decrees' that would start things rolling.

He began by an intense programme of building rows upon rows of solar panels in fields around the country. More wind farms were built along with the introduction of wave power farms generating electricity that were established at appropriate areas of the coast.

Solar, Wind and Waves became the motto for the new National Electricity Authority. This was fine and was welcomed by the people. It provided new jobs and work for those that had lost their jobs when the UK crashed out of the European Union in 2020 causing many companies to become bankrupt and close.

Secondary he wanted all petrol and diesel fuelled vehicles to be replaced by electric powered vehicles within a specific time frame of five years. He did not see why some families had one car but more well off families had several. He felt this was a matter of inequality and should be rectified. Therefore only one car per household would be allowed. This would help in reducing harmful emissions and help everyone to feel more equal.

The head of each household would be responsible for complying with this by ensuring that excess vehicles were surrendered to designated collection points. In addition only the vehicle with the lowest emissions was to be retained for the families use. It was argued that the time allocated for this would not be long enough for the population to adapt to the new regulation but he was adamant that this should go ahead and issued a Royal Decree to this effect.

Thirdly a big contributor to air pollution was congestion in the cities and motorways and the King was well aware of this. The problem being that there were too many vehicles on the road at the same time. Just one small incident could bring vehicles to a standstill that may last for hours during which time drivers would leave the engines of their cars and Lorries ticking over poisoning the air with exhaust fumes. Therefore until all petrol and diesel vehicles were off the road, a restriction on their use would be imposed on the owners.

Reorganisation of Vehicle Registration was made a priority. All vehicles were given a new code to be etched onto its windscreen. Only on certain days of the week would the vehicles with the appropriate code of the day be allowed onto the roads. The present network of CCTV cameras and vehicle congestion cameras would check compliance with the new regulation. Those found guilty of ignoring the regulation would have their vehicle seized and crushed without redress. Businesses would have to find a way to address this.

In the past the Prince's Trust and the Prince's Charities Foundation had helped many people to lead a better more fulfilled life. Now King Charles wanted the country that he now ruled to be a happy country with everyone helping his or her neighbour and repairing the rift caused by BREXIT. He tasked his advisers to come up with ideas on how to achieve this.

They all agreed that Social Engineering similar to what CHINA had introduced to its people would be a way of achieving this.

This 'carrot and stick' system meant that the population would be rewarded for all the good deeds that they did and punished for any bad behaviour. At the initial start of the system everyone on the population database would be issued with 1000 points. For good deeds points would be added and for bad behaviour points would be subtracted. The more points that you collected the more rewards you would gain, such as higher on the housing list or more speedy access to health care on waiting lists. Points could be deducted for offences like speeding, petty crime or other unsocial offences.

The system would require a lot more CCTV cameras to be positioned so that everyone could be monitored at all times.
 This in turn would create work in manufacturing the cameras and hardware and jobs in installing the system and maintaining it.

After much deliberation the King was leaning towards implementing such a system but he had doubts about how the British people would react to it and hesitated before giving it a green light. However word of his intention had leaked out and mutterings from the people were beginning to be heard. The population did not like the idea of being under twenty four hour surveillance.

The King had for many years had an interest in the English Civil War and had often wondered what it would have been like to stand alongside the Royalist army on the battlefield as his ancestor had. He knew of course of the Sealed Knot Society and their re-enactments and it was while browsing their web site on his Laptop that he saw a re-enactment of the Battle of Naseby was due to take place this coming June.

This might just be his last chance to take part in one. He wasn't getting any younger and while he was still capable of riding a horse, having been a keen polo player, he did not want to leave it much later. With the anniversary of the battle of Naseby soon approaching this would be ideal time to fulfil his ambition. So finally deciding to take part in the re-enactment as King Charles I he summoned his secretary and asked what his commitments during that month were. The re-enactment was due to take place over the weekend of the 10th and 11th of June and as he had no pressing engagements at that time things looked good.

He informed his secretary of his intentions and as it was now late February, he instructed him to get things moving.

His advisers tried to persuade him against taken part but the King felt that this would be his last chance he would have of experiencing what it must have been like to stand on the battlefield, the same as his ancestors did facing his enemies. He would be mounted on his horse to the rear of the main line of troops so wouldn't be too close to the milling about on the battlefield and should be relatively safe. Besides he would also have his bodyguards beside him as well.

His staff began contacting the various agencies that would be involved including the local council, the Sealed Knot Society, the Police and the Security Services. They in turn informed the departments within their organization that would be involved. Everyone was sworn to secrecy for the safety of the King in these unsettled times was paramount.

Chapter 7

A Secret Shared is a Secret Lost

It was in March during one of his visits to Thames House in London that Mark was briefed of the Kings intention to take part in the forthcoming re-enactment at Naseby and advised that a red alert should be put in place for the duration of the time he was there. At a meeting of the Joint Intelligence Agency it had been agreed that this was a most likely time that an attempt on the King's life would be made and that all precautions must be put in place.

The management of the Sealed Knot Society had also received official communication from the palace of the King's intention and would they therefore make great effort to put on the largest re-enactment possible.

This in turn was passed down to Mark in his capacity of National Events Organiser who immediately called for a meeting of all of the local area organisers throughout the country. This group was unofficially known as the' Inner Circle of the Sealed Knot 'where most decisions of the Society were made. The meeting was held in the Victory Services Club in London that is quite near to Marble

Arch. Most of the delegates were ex-servicemen so were able to book rooms at the club and make an enjoyable 'boys' weekend of it.

At the meeting held in the 'El-Alamein' room of the Club Mark explained to those present of the King's wishes to act as King Charles 1 at the next re-enactment. He asked that those who usually take the King's part ensure that Charles should be well briefed as to how he should act out his part. He stressed that the local organisers should encourage as many of their members to attend and take part in the forth-coming re-enactment. He also stressed the requirement for security and asked that no one should discuss any of this outside of this meeting.

One of those present at the meeting was Edward Okey who represented the Leicester Branch of the society. He always took part in the re-enactments as a Parliamentarian and did his best to encourage others to do the same. One of his distant ancestors was Colonel John Okey, a commander of the New Model Army's Regiment of Dragoons who had fought so well at Naseby. Edward took great pleasure in letting everyone that he met know of this fact sometimes to the bored derision of his fellow Society members.

Edward's marriage was not going too well. The children had long since left home and established themselves with a life elsewhere. After thirty years both he and his wife had drifted apart and led their own lives and interests. They had little left in common. She had her friends and her Facebook that she spent most of her time on. Edward's retirement did not bide well and he used his time with the Society as an excuse to get away from her and took the opportunity whenever he could. His evenings were mostly spent in his local pub where he could indulge in banter with other men as men do.

It was just after he returned from his trip to London and his briefing about the King's intended attendance at the upcoming re-enactment that he paid his usual visit to his local, the White Bull.

"Evening Ted." The Landlord greeted him. "Thought you was ill or something, you not being in these last few nights."

"Had to go to an important meeting in London." He replied. "Got a big re-enactment coming up? A special one this one." He straightened up, making himself look and feel important.

"What do you mean special?" asked the Landlord.

"Not allowed to say." replied Edward.

"Alright keep it to yourself then. Not really interested anyway." The Landlord moved away to serve another customer.

Hopkins who was standing near to Edward had listened to the conversation and wanted to know more. Moving closer to Edward he pretended to trip and stumbled into Edward knocking over his drink.

"Sorry friend." He apologized. "Must have slipped on that wet patch. Here let me get you another beer."

Edward was muttering to himself as he wiped himself down with a bar towel but allowed a fresh drink to be placed before him.

The two of them got talking and took turns at buying a round. Edward enjoyed the other man's company; it was good to have someone to talk with. The drink loosed his tongue and he let slip about King Charles taking part in the forthcoming re-enactment. Edward said laughingly that he hoped they would be allowed to chase the King off the battlefield just as his ancestor had. The germ of an idea began to grow in Hopkins mind. This would be perhaps the ideal opportunity to get rid of the King.

After a while Hopkins realized that there was no further information to be had went to look for one of the RGB leaders to tell them what he had learned.

Finding both Ritchie and Jimmy in a corner of the Bar Hopkins began to outline what he had heard.

"This may prove to be our greatest opportunity to bring an end to an unjust rule and establish RGB as the new parliament." He ended.

"Hush." said Ritchie looking around him "You never know whose listening. Tell you what, let's go around to your digs and hear what you've got to say there."

And with that the three of them left the White Bull.

Once at Hopkins bedsit they checked to see that they were alone and once satisfied that there was no one else present told Hopkins to tell them of his idea.

"I believe that re-enactments are choreographed but sometimes can be difficult to manage. This would give us chance of getting close to the King and making sure he would not survive an attempt on his life. It would require dedicated men who would be prepared to die along with the victim as there would minimal chance of escape."

"But how could someone get close with a weapon without being seen? Ritchie asked him.

"The only way," Hopkins reasoned, "would be if that someone were to be part of the re-enactment party itself. As for the weapon some of the re-enactment would be armed with muskets and while these wouldn't be accurate or powerful enough for the purpose a musket could perhaps be modified that would do the job."

The two leaders listened and after Hopkins had finished agreed that it might just be possible with some planning and finding some men who would be prepared to take the risk that it might just succeed.

Without hesitation Hopkins volunteered himself and his two companions to be the ideal choice as they had the skills and the knowledge of what would be required.

"OK." said Ritchie, "We'll give it some thought. Don't discuss this with anyone else. Security must be of the essence. If even a whisper of this got to the Security Services it would be a non-starter."

The two men left and once out of the building Ritchie asked Jimmy what did he think of Hopkins plan.

"I think that it has a good chance of succeeding." replied Jimmy. "It has the makings of a sound plan and it's simple with not much to go wrong. Yes let's go for it." He finished off. "We'll need someone to see to the weapon. Have you any ideas who could do what we need?" asked Ritchie.

"I do as a matter of fact." said Jimmy. "While I was up in Newcastle I had an old German Luger pistol that required some repair. I was put in touch with an ex RAF guy who done a marvellous job and made it just like new. I'm sure this would be just up his street. I'll get back to him and see what he has to say."

"There is something else" said Ritchie "I think this would be the chance of establishing RGB as the ruling party of the UK. If Hopkins succeeds we could storm Westminster and seize control of Parliament before anyone realized what had happened and any action taken. What do you think?"

Jimmy thought before replying. "And who is going to be the one who takes over the running of the country once we succeed?" Who will be 'El Presidento'?" he added with a trace of sarcasm. "Why me, who else?" replied Ritchie "On behalf of the two of us of course." he added smiling. "If you look after the operational side of things then I'll do the administration, so as to speak."

Jimmy laughed, "I should have known. OK let's do it. I'll look after getting things moving."

The RGB meeting was held as usual upstairs in the storage come meeting room of the White Bull. There were twelve men, each one an Area Controller, attending this meeting including Hopkins and the two leaders. Ritchie and Jimmy took up their places at one end of the table while the others found their own places on the chairs at either side. Outside the room door stood a burly six-foot member of RGB ensuring that no one attempted to eavesdrop on what was being discussed.

But walls 'do have ears' and on the walls of the meeting room the cameras and microphones of the spiders began sending their data to a device in the holdall of a man distributing religious leaflets outside of the pub which then relayed the data to the Security Services Network.

After hearing the various reports from the delegates and colleting the monies that they had brought from their various questionable activities, Ritchie told everyone to keep quiet as he had some important business to discuss.

"A strong organisation such as ours must be able to act as the time and opportunity present themselves. Therefore I want all areas in towns and villages to be able to take over from local councils and Police forces if required. This will take careful planning and training in readiness. You as Area Controllers will ensure that your areas will be capable of this when and if called upon. Do I make myself clear?" There was a muttered agreement and nodding of heads around the table. "Start making arrangements now so that when I say go, we can all act together as one. I want you to report back to me at the earliest that all is ready before the end of next month."

Jimmy rose to his feet as Ritchie sat down.

"Yes, there might soon be a great opportunity to strike a decisive blow for what we all want." he informed the room.
"I won't go into full details because of security. But what I want is ideas on how we can get some small items into an open air public display like a music festival without any problems." He said looking into the faces of the seated men.
"So who's first with a master plan?" he asked.

There was a hushed silence as each man looked at the others hoping for some inspiration.

"Security is always tight at these types of events ever since that business with 'Al Qaeda' a few years ago. There'll be body searches before you get in to the arena. They would soon find anything that you weren't supposed to have and there would be sniffer dogs for any whiff of explosives. They're good them dogs could sniff a bullet hidden up a fishes arse hole." Volunteered one man.

"OK" said Jimmy. "Go and have a drink and have a think about it. Be back here in half an hour. Bring your pints back here if you want and no talking outside of this room about what you've heard."

The men eventually returned and took up their places. Several ideas were discussed before being rejected.

"One more thing," Jimmy told the seated men "I want you all to organize your members to take part in a planned protest in London on the 10th of June. Further details will be sent by text as usual. I want as many people there as you can muster. So get started."

"What will we be protesting about?" asked one of the men. "Anything that you want to." replied Jimmy to the laughter of the others.

As the meeting began to disperse Richie called Mike Bradley, the London Area Controller over.

"Mike" he began "There's a special job I want you to organise."

"Yeah and what's that Richie?" Mike asked.

"I don't want to discuss it here in case some of the others overhear. Come on I'll walk with you to the rail station." Ritchie replied looking around him.

They both left the pub and making sure no one was within hearing distance Richie began to brief Mike on what was wanted of him.

"I want you and your lads to keep tabs on where Charlie boy's off springs are and when I give the OK on the 10th June I want you to go in and seize them. Take them somewhere secure and look after them. OK?"

"For how long?" Mike asked.

"Until I say. Any other questions? No. Good, let me know if there are any problems. Just one other thing, have you any of our men working in Westminster Palace?" Richie asked

"I couldn't say for sure Richie." Mike replied "But I can check when I get back and let you know. If that's ok? Why what do you want?" He finished off.

"What I want is for some guns to be made available to a team of our boys from inside the palace. Do you think that you could organise getting some inside?"

"Anything's possible. Just give me a bit of time and I'll see what I can come up with and I'll get back to you."
"Fine, "replied Richie "But don't leave it for too long. I want everything setup for the 10th June when we have the demo in London."

Leaving the London Controller to think about what had been said Ritchie returned to the White Bull to let Jimmy know that he had told Mike what was expected of him at the London end.

Chapter 8

Whitley Bay

Gerry Marshall had completed twenty-two years with the RAF as an Armourer and had retired to Whitley Bay, a small town on the east coast of England near to Newcastle.

He had purchased a small but powerful lathe with his gratuity and set it up in his garage. It enabled him to keep his skills up to date and do various jobs for his friends.

As time went on he set up a small business repairing antiques and became well known for repairing old weapons including muskets and swords.

Gerry was a Republican through and through. His time spent in the services with all of the bull and being told what to do by leaders whom he had no respect for and who he considered less fit to hold their position's than the one he held, had diminished his thoughts of loyalty to the crown.

When friends asked him to carry out repairs or alterations on objects that might not be considered lawful, he was quite willing to oblige. So when RGB learned of Gerry's leanings and skills he was invited to become an active member, which he accepted,

Jimmy had caught the train to Newcastle on the first leg of his journey. Leaving the train at Newcastle Central Station he crossed over the road to a corner café and bought himself a meal of egg, chips and beans. He carefully observed anyone that followed him into the café checking out any likely suspects that might be Security Services. Finishing his meal he paid and left the café checking again to see if he was being followed. Making his way to the Eldon Square Bus Station he caught a bus that took him over the River Tyne to the Felling area of Gateshead.

Craig Adams stood six feet three inches tall. He was of muscular build; his broad arms and upper body were covered in tattoos as were his lower legs and with a close shaved head gave the appearance of someone you would not wish to mess with. Craig worked evenings as a doorman at one of Newcastle's most popular nightspots. He was also the North East Controller for the RGB. He had been warned to expect Jimmy to discuss some important business.

Jimmy got off the bus at the Sunderland Road stop and made his way through the labyrinth of alleyways' and streets of a new housing estate until he came to Craig's address. He was greeted by Craig and ushered inside.

"Nice to see you again Jimmy. How's things with you?" he asked. "It's been a while since you were last up this way. Got more Demos' planned?" he smiled.

"Not this time Craig." Jimmy replied.

They had both been involved in earlier demonstrations and marches by the English Defence League through Newcastle and running confrontations against the Police and opposing groups.

"Do you remember that guy at Whitley Bay? Him who fixed that Luger that I had. Is he still around and with us?" He asked.

"You mean Gerry; yes he's helping us out with the odd job now and then." Craig answered.

"Good. I don't want to go into details. This has to be strictly 'need to know' business, I'm sure you'll understand, but we might have to call on his services." Jimmy told him.

"That's OK I know what you mean." Replied Craig "The less people that know the better security. But it must be something big I bet. Anyway you can kip down here tonight, I've prepared the spare room for you and we can visit Gerry tomorrow."

The next morning they both made their way down to Felling Metro Station and didn't have long to wait for the next train to Whitley Bay via Newcastle.

They left the Metro Station at Whitley Bay and made their way to a well-established quiet residential area. They turned into one of the streets where most of the detached houses had large gardens with six or seven feet high conifers providing security and privacy around their perimeter.

"This is ours." stated Craig, stopping before a wrought iron gate. He reached over and pressed a button on an intercom that was set into one of the gates brick pillars.

After a short wait they were rewarded with a muffled metallic voice "Who is it and what do you want?" asked the voice.

"Here to see my good friend Gerry on a personal matter. He knows me from the Newcastle night club and from Gateshead." replied Craig.

After a short while the wrought iron gate slid to one side allowing them to enter and then closed again once they were inside.

Gerry, a middle aged man approaching fifty and beginning to put on weight around his middle, stood at the front door of the house. He greeted them both before leading them into the house and along a dimly lit passageway into a sitting room.

Bidding his two visitors to sit Gerry asked if they would like anything to drink. Receiving a negative shakes of the heads from both he asked.

"What do I owe this visit for then? It must be something important to bring you both here. It must be ten years or so since I last saw you Jimmy when I fixed that old Luger of yours."

"That's right," Replied Jimmy "but I've got an important task I think you'll be able to do and I want you to speak about it to no one but me."

95

"Sounds ominous," answered Gerry smiling "let's be hearing it then."

"Before I tell you the requirements." Jimmy turned to Craig. "Craig would you mind leaving the room and make sure no one outside listens in."

Craig left closing the door as he went and positioned himself half way along the passageway.

Jimmy looked at Gerry and began his cover story about the requirements. "There is a film maker who has been supplying money to one of the Royalist organizations who we require to be taken out. Permanently." he added.
"He intends to make a film about the English Civil War. We thought the best way of achieving the objective would be during one of the battle scenes when the Musketeers fire off a volley. So what we require of you is to supply us with a weapon capable of the task. What do you say?" He finished off.

"Sounds feasible." replied Gerry. "What sort of distance between the target and the shooter?"

"Could be anything between one to three hundred meters," Jimmy answered. "Perhaps less perhaps more."

"Well that lets out a Musket. It wouldn't be accurate enough at that range. They were only useful when fired in volleys by groups of men with not much hope of hitting anything they aimed at. Let me have a little think about it and see if I can come up with anything. Call Craig back and I'll go and check with my wife if she can rustle up some lunch. Not be long." Gerry left to organize the lunch and to think about how it could be done.

Gerry's wife was used to organizing quick meals. After spending most of her life in RAF camps around the world she was used to unexpected guests dropping in.

After lunch Gerry invited Jimmy to join him in the garden where they could not be overheard.

"There's one way that I think we could do this and that would require a higher velocity rifle. A 5.56 rifle would do it but it would have to be disguised as a Musket and they only fire single shots. Can you get me an AR15 rifle or at least a barrel off one and a carton of 5.56 rounds?" He asked.

"I'm sure one can be found." replied Jimmy. "If we get one to you how long would it take you to come up with the finished goods?"

"Three or four weeks should be enough time." Gerry answered.

With that agreement Craig and Jimmy took their leave. Craig returned to Gateshead and Jimmy caught the train from Newcastle Central Station back to Leicester.

Word via the dark-web was circulated to all RGB Area Controllers that an AR15 rifle and ammunition was required and that it was urgent.

Chapter 9

The American Connection

Leroy Walter Kitelinger was of Jewish European decent. Prior to the Second World War his family had become alarmed at the way Hitler and his National Party were speaking of the 'Jewish Problem'. They had both managed to board a ship travelling to America and settled in New York.

Leroy was a late unplanned child to his elderly parents. When they both died within a short time of each other Leroy was taken into Juvenile Care. As soon as he was old enough he had enlisted in the USAF and had served in many of the locations where American troops were stationed.

He was quick to learn and had gradually risen to the rank of Master Warrant Officer. He was now the Senior American Armaments Technician at RAF Milldenvale and was responsible for all Ordnance on the station that was assigned to American personnel.

A little known fact is that there is also a small discreet armoury of unlisted weapons that were not part of an official inventory. The weapons were untraceable, as they had been specially manufactured to conceal their place of origin or history.

The weapons were held in a secure World War II concrete bunker at the far side of the airfield. Only Leroy and the Station Commander knew about this secret armoury and access was only granted to those with special clearance. This hidden armoury was for use by members of Delta Force, America's top-secret soldiers similar to the UK's SAS. There were occasions when Delta Force or the CIA were required to carry our covert operations in mainland Europe and required specialist weapons. This is where they were supplied from.

Leroy was near to completing his time with the Air force. With a view to the future he was trying to build up his funds to supplement his Air Force pension for when he retired. Apart from his Air force pay Leroy also had a secondary means of income and that was supplying drugs to some of the station personnel. He had an established supply from another dealer in Cambridge and would drive there on his days off replenish his stock.

The dealer in Cambridge, Len Markam was a member of RGB so when the call came from RGB central for the requirements for an AR15 type rifle and ammunition Len thought that he had the answer. Len got back to RGB central to let them know that he could possibly supply if his source would play ball. Jimmy replied that he must ensure that he could supply without fail.

Len contacted Leroy to let him know that he had just received a special consignment of Cocaine that was selling fast and did he want any of it. Of course Leroy did and when could he have it. Len arranged to meet Leroy in Cambridge outside of the Guildhall on Market Hill at 12 o' clock sharp the following day.

 Leroy dressed in a dark blue bomber jacket and grey corduroy trousers arrived at the meeting place and with time to spare paid for a coffee from a street stall and sat down on a nearby bench waiting for Len to arrive. He looked around at the people in the street, checking if there were any Police about or any other servicemen that might recognize him and wonder what he was doing here.

Leroy checked his watch, Len was late. He would finish his coffee and if Len hadn't shown up he would arrange a meeting at a later date. No use in taking chances.

Just then Len appeared from around the corner and seeing Leroy came and sat down next to him.

"Bit late aren't you Len, what kept you?" Leroy asked.

"Sorry Leroy. I had some trouble with some plain clothes coppers following me but I think I've managed to shake them off." Len replied as he adjusted the peak of his cap lower over his eyes.

Leroy looked around him again checking out the people moving about but all he saw were the same market traders and some tourists taken photographs of the Guild Hall.

As he turned back Len lowered his head and thrust a small parcel wrapped in cellophane into Leroy's hands. Leroy instinctively took hold of the parcel and then realizing what it must be quickly unzipped his bomber jacket and hid the parcel inside it.

"What are you doing?" he asked Len in a hushed but angry voice. "Someone might have seen what you did and twigged on what it was."

"It's OK." said Len "No one saw us at least no one that matters."

"OK." replied Leroy "Let's settle up and I'll be on my way. Usual price is it?" he asked.

Leroy reached into his jacket pocket and pulled out a thick envelope containing a wad of banknotes to pay Len. Len took his time in accepting the envelope and when he did he tore it open and checked the notes inside.

"There's something else this time Leroy. This time I want a gun and I know you can supply it." Len told him.

Leroy was stunned "I've got no guns." he said.

"Perhaps not personally but I'm sure you can get one." Len stated, "The kind that I'm looking for is one of your Military rifles and a carton of 5.56 shells. If that's too difficult I'll settle for the barrel only. But you'll have to hurry because I can't wait for very long."

"You're crazy man. How could I possibly get one of those?" Leroy protested.

Just then Len's mobile phone rang. He looked at it for a moment and then spoke into it. "OK got it."

Len looked at Leroy and spoke softly to him.
"I want what I asked for delivered to me by the end of next week otherwise."

He let Leroy see what was playing on the mobile's screen. It was a replay of Leroy accepting a package from Len and Len getting paid.

"Now what would your Security staff think when they receive a copy of this video along with the title 'American serviceman caught dealing drugs'? Or the British Police for that matter? You have till next Friday to deliver."

And with that Len got up and left accompanied by the couple that had masqueraded as tourists who had taken the video.

Leroy remained sitting on the bench for a while stunned by what he had been told to do. It would cost him his job if he were found out. The end of his career in the Air force, his pension and he would probably go to prison as well.

But if he didn't do as Len wanted and the video went viral the same would happen. He thought long and hard. There was just one possibility. If he did what Len wanted and used one of the spare barrels from the 'Delta stock' there was just the chance that he could be retired and away from RAF Milldenvale and the Air Force before anyone checked the store. Then he could drop out of sight.

Finishing his coffee Leroy threw the empty cardboard cup at the refuse bin but missed it. He became aware of the stallholder watching him and hurriedly picked up the cup and placed it in the bin. He didn't want to give the stallholder any reason to remember him by.

It was two days later that Leroy made his way across the airfield to the concrete bunker. It was the same day that he regularly carried out an inspection of the bunker so it was nothing out of the ordinary.

Once inside he made sure the door was secured and went to carry out his checks only this time it was for a suitable weapon as requested by Len.

Unlike most military armouries where the weapons are kept in open racks and secured by a chain running through their finger guards all the weapons in the bunker were kept in locked steel boxes, each one being numbered. Some boxes contained Rifles others sub machine guns, other a selection of handguns including semi-automatics and revolvers. A selection of grenades including stun, fragmentation, smoke, phosphorus and tear gas were available if required. Only Leroy had the master list indicating which box held what weapon. Reaching a pile of four crates he unlocked the top box and drew out the spare barrel of an assault rifle. He wrapped the barrel in some track suit trousers before placing it into a canvas bag amongst some other gym clothing and relocked the box. He then restacked the boxes with the one containing the rifle minus its spare barrel at the bottom of the pile. Taking the canvas bag Leroy relocked the bunker and drove back to his quarters with the rifle barrel.

On the Thursday of the following week Leroy delivered a spare barrel from one of the new generation M23 Squad Automatic Rifles chambered for a pressure of 60-80 KPS (Kilo pounds per Square inch) along with two cartons of the newly issued steel jacket 5.56mm rounds to Len.

One of Len's men standing by with a high powered Triumph motor bike was then handed the canvas holdall containing the requested item, less the gym clothing, and told to deliver it to an address in Leicester. Jimmy himself collected the holdall from the address and using a friend's car drove to Whitely Bay and delivered the holdall to Gerry. Job done. It was up to Gerry now to come up with the required item.

Chapter 10

The Finished Article

Gerry got to works straight away remembering his promise to have the job done within four weeks.

He had acquired a single shot break type shotgun and removed the butt and attachments from the barrel and stock. He removed the fore sight from the newly acquired M23 barrel so that it gave the appearance of a hollow steel tube.

Using the butt end of the shotgun Gerry modified it to be attached to the barrel. By means of a concealed catch the complete rifle would be allowed to break open the same as a shotgun with just enough space to insert a round into the breech. This would allow the existing hammer to be moved centre slightly so as not to be noticed by anything other than a detailed inspection, enabling the hammer to strike the percussion cap of the loaded round.

As it did not resemble anything like a Flintlock Musket of the Civil War period Gerry wound layers of fiberglass around the steel barrel until it was of the correct diameter and length. He then stained it in the true colours of a Musket and added some finishing touches. All that was needed now was test firing the finished article.

It was early morning that Gerry loaded his LandRover with the modified rifle concealed in a rolled up carpet and a day rucksack containing a flask of coffee, some cheese sandwiches and a carton of 5.56 mm rounds.

He travelled north along the A19 towards Morpeth until turning off for Belsay and onwards to Otterburn where the army was very active and had several firing ranges.

At a shop in the village he purchased a replica army camouflaged jacket and a forage cap as well as a Figure 11 target. If he was challenged he would claim to be one of the Range Wardens but with a bit of luck he would be done and away without anyone seeing him or taken any notice of what he was doing.

Leaving the village he drove along a secondary road until he spotted a rutted track leading off to his right. Turning onto it he bounced along the winding track up onto the moors until he came upon a shallow re-entrant between some low hills that was ideal for his purpose. Gerry set up the Figure 11 target and paced out one hundred meters, two hundred meters and three hundred meters, marking each distance with a small wooden stake.

He began with his first shot at one hundred meters. The sharp crack from the rifle was muffled by the low hills on either side. There was very little recoil from the rifle even though the ammunition was of the new higher velocity issue. He checked the target. The rifle was firing a bit low. He adjusted the sights and fired again. This time he had made a head shot with his second round. He tried again from three hundred meters while sitting on the ground and steadying his elbows on his knees. The second hole in the target was only slightly to the side of the first. One more for luck he thought and fired a third time. Three head shots on the target. Not bad shooting he thought especially aiming with open sights. Satisfied he collected the target and the used cartridges, loaded up the LandRover and left the empty moor.

After returning to his home Gerry had one more task to do before he contacted Jimmy to inform him that his task was complete and that was to modify a few rounds.

He carefully drilled several millimetres into the points of some rounds making them hollow. Because the modified Musket would only fire one round at a time it was important that the first shot would cause the most damage. There might not be the opportunity for a second shot. Drilling out the bullet would ensure the round burst on impact ensuring maximum damage to the target.

Setting three of these rounds to one side he carefully inserted a small measure of the poison Ricin sealing the tips with sealing wax. He marked these three rounds with a red marker pen. If the target was only wounded the Ricin would ensure that a kill would be achieved. The other hollowed out rounds would be available for the shooter to practice with and they also had their tips sealed with wax.

A message was sent to Jimmy saying that his item was ready for collection.

Since his last meeting with Gerry, Jimmy had not been idle. He had discussed the problem of getting high velocity rounds passed sniffer dogs with Ritchie. The dogs were trained to ignore the 'Black Powder' that the Musketeers carried but it was highly likely that the modern explosive in the cartridges would be 'sniffed out'. They couldn't take the chance of carrying them on their person or that would be show over.

Ritchie thought that the only safe way would be to smuggle them in somehow and then collect them once inside the grounds of the re-enactment. He asked some of his men for ideas.
One of them had in the past taped drugs in one of the pre-stressed mobile steel toilets, known as Portaloo's, to get it into one of the

big open-air summer music festivals. He had sealed it in a plastic bag and then wrapped it in absorbent cloth before finally dousing it with a strong disinfectant. The 'Portaloo's always stank of disinfectant so a little more did not raise any concerns.

Ritchie liked the idea and conferred with Jimmy. Their only concern was that taping the ammunition onto the Portaloo would not be secure enough and the rounds might be lost.
Jimmy agreed to take on the finer points of the project and would keep Ritchie updated on their progress.

Jimmy sent for one of his top men Billy Morrison, whom he could rely upon to do some scouting at the intended Naseby site.
Billy was one of the many car workers who had lost their jobs after BREXIT when Nisan closed their Sunderland plant and moved their car production to mainland Europe. Billy like others drifted south looking for work and had become involved with the RGB.

Billy was given a short brief on what was intended and told to find out which company would be supplying Portaloo's at the Naseby re-enactment. He was to get a job with them and see if he could come up with any ideas on smuggling in a few rounds of ammunition.

Billy booked in for Bed and Breakfast at a local pub in Market Harborough that was not far from Naseby. He let it be known to the Landlord that he was looking for work and did he know of any that was going. The Landlord said that he would ask around and let him know if he heard anything.

While checking the list of jobs available at the local Job Centre Billy had found out that a local firm had the contract for supplying the Naseby site with the mobile toilets and for tiding the site up afterwards.

He approached the firm's office and asked about employment. "I heard that you will be busy next month at the Naseby show and wondered if there was any work going?" he asked the secretary.

"You might just be in luck.' She replied. "Our regular driver is about to retire. I'm just typing a job advert for the local paper. Wait here and I'll see what Paul has to say. You do drive don't you?" She asked as an afterthought.

"Yes among many things." Billy answered smiling at her.

The secretary was gone for only a few minutes and returned accompanied by an older man who was obviously Paul the owner.

"Looking for work are you?" Paul asked him. "Can you drive a lorry?"

"Yes no problem." replied Billy "Used to do local deliveries around Birmingham and City to City trunk runs with BRS."

"Are you the man staying at our local? Jake said he knew someone who was staying with him was looking for work." Paul asked.

"Yes that must be me. I let him know that I was after work." Billy answered.

"OK then. You look fit enough to me. Let's see what your driving's like first and then if it's ok we can see about a job. Only temporary to begin with mind, and cash in hand. Does that sound reasonable?"

"That sounds just fine to me." replied Billy and was told to report the following morning at eight o'clock sharp.

Billy wasted to time in contacting Ritchie to let him know the news. Ritchie congratulated him and told him to stay there and keep his eyes and ears open for anything that might prove useful. He would contact him later.

Jimmy had been waiting anxiously to hear from Gerry in Whitley Bay so when he received a message that all was go he was very relieved.

He also discussed with Gerry that the men chosen for the job would require some practice with the modified rifle to ensure they would hit the target.

"No problem," replied Gerry, "bring them up here and we'll sort things out."

Next on the list was organising the right men for the job. He contacted Hopkins and asked if he and his two companions were still prepared to take part in what they had previously discussed. Hopkins answered that he and his men were ready to do what was required.

"Ok then pack your kit for an overnight trip up north. Go and kit yourselves out at the Army and Navy Stores with some army combat type uniform so you could pass as soldiers." Jimmy instructed. "Be prepared to leave this coming Friday. We'll leave Friday evening and drive overnight. Any questions?" There were no questions. Hopkins left to prepare his two men for the trip and to get some ex-army kit as instructed.

Jimmy had arranged to meet Gerry at a Garden Centre near to Newcastle airport where they could breakfast and have a wash and brush up.

Gerry was already at the Garden Centre when they arrived.
"So you made it then." He greeted the four men. "Let's go inside and have some food."
They found a table where they could discuss the day's activities without being overheard.

Gerry had chosen a Saturday because there was plenty movement of part time soldiers and vehicles travelling on their intended route at weekends, so they shouldn't be noticed as anything different. He instructed them to change into the army kit that they had purchased and leave their other clothes in Jimmy's car. They would all travel in Gerry's LandRover, as it looked more military. Jimmy's car would remain at the Garden Centre where they could pick it up on their return journey.

Gerry retraced his previous journey to the re-entrant and found that the distance markers still in place as he had left them.

After checking around the area they unloaded the modified musket from the LandRover and set up the Figure 11 target. Gerry began

115

giving them instructions on the weapon and asked who would be the actual marksman on the day.

It had been decided that Nathan who, in his previous life, used to be a gamekeeper on a large estate and acted as the troop sharpshooter when called upon would do the actual firing, while Benjamin would act as reserve and protect Nathan if required. As they only had a limited supply of ammunition they did not want to waste it needlessly so it was decided to concentrate on Nathan's accuracy.

They began at one hundred meters and after a few shots Nathan was hitting the target without fail. There was very little recoil from the weapon and it felt well balanced. The hits were quite good at two hundred meters as well but when they moved to three hundred meters the accuracy fell away.

Gerry instructed them to lie down on the ground when firing at that range to improve the accuracy but because they would be firing from a line of standing men on the actual day it would not be possible.

Jimmy then told Benjamin to stand in front of Nathan so that he could rest and steady the rifle on Benjamin's shoulder. That worked fine and Nathan was soon hitting the target with each shot. They decided that on the actual day this would be the procedure that they would adopt no matter what the distance.

Once they were all satisfied that the rifle with Nathan firing would do the job they began tiding up the firing range collecting the spent cartridges removing the Figure 11 target and the marker stakes.

After loading the LandRover with the bits of equipment Gerry took Jimmy to one side.

"Here Jimmy take these." Gerry produced a tobacco tin and on opening it showed it to Jimmy. Inside cushioned by cotton wool, were the three 5.56mm rounds that Gerry had marked with a red felt tipped pen around the brass cartridge cases.

"Just in case your intended target is only wounded. If they are," he continued, "then these will ensure that they won't recover. I've modified these three rounds to a hollow point.

Because you can only fire one round at a time you want to ensure a kill. These rounds will burst on impact ensuring maximum damage to the target. I've also inserted a small quantity of Ricin into the hollow point to ensure a kill would be achieved. Just make sure the wax on the point covering the hole doesn't come lose. Otherwise it's the marksman who'd be in trouble."

Jimmy closed the tin's lid and carefully put it into his pocket. They drove back to the Garden Centre, said goodbye to Gerry, collected their car and returned to Leicester.

Chapter 11

Final Preparations

With only a short time left before the re-enactment was due to take place a flurry of activity was underway by all those involved.

While Ritchie would be in London at the planned demonstration and the intended occupation of Westminster Palace Jimmy didn't want to be left out of the action. He would listen out for Ritchie's call for 'Go' and lead the Leicester team in taking over the City's Council Offices. He had arranged for all of his assault team to meet up at the White Bull where they would wait and be ready for Ritchie's signal and leave from there.

Jimmy wasted no time in contacting Billy and arranged to meet him at Rutland Water Park where they could discuss what was required of him.

Rutland Water Park was a recreation area more or less halfway between Jimmy and Billy's locations. Covering a large area there were plenty of places where they could discuss and finalize their plans on how to get the rounds into the Naseby re-enactment arena without them being discovered. Security was going to be tight so there had to be a fool proof way of getting them in.

"Have you come up with any ideas?" Jimmy asked. "We need to get this moving. Time is getting tight." He finished off.

"Yea, I've been thinking about this and come to the conclusion that sometimes it's best to hide something in plain view of those that's doing the searching." Billy stated looking at Jimmy for agreement.

"Like what do you have in mind?" asked Jimmy.

"There's some Disabled Portaloo's being sent to the re-enactment. Inside there's black ventilation pipe near to the toilet seat that goes up the wall to the roof. It's quite wide and causes a bit of a shadow on one side. If we had some black tubing the same diameter as the rounds or slightly wider we could put the rounds inside it and superglue it alongside the length of the ventilation pipe as if it was part of the fittings. We could seal the tubing at both ends making it airtight so that no dogs could smell the explosive in the rounds. What do you think?" Billy asked.

Jimmy thought for a few moments before replying. "I think it might just work. OK let's go for it. The whole project depends on getting the rounds through so the marksman can collect them. We'd better not fail."

He reached in to his pocket and passed the tin containing the three modified round to Billy.

"These are the rounds Billy. Be careful how you handle them. Don't let the wax on the ends come loose or you'll not live to regret it."

He finished off by telling Billy what they contained.

With the final points decided upon Billy would contact Jimmy once everything was in place and how to identify the Portaloo containing the ammunition.

That left Jimmy with one more thing to organise and that was how to get the three assassins into the re-enactment arena.

Four weeks prior to the re-enactment the army had thrown a cordon around the Naseby site. No one was allowed to enter without a special clearance and only after being checked out by the Security Services. This was so that no concealed explosive devices could be left hidden to be remotely detonated at an appropriate time. Anyone enquiring was told it was an army exercise on internal security. Discreet but methodical checks on all of the local population were carried out paying particular attention to anyone who was not originally from the area or had recently moved in.

Back in Hexham the long winter months had been slow in passing. It seemed as if the seasons were becoming more extreme and that spring and autumn were becoming shorter. Most folk agreed that this was due to global warming. This winter had been an exceptionally hard one but Daniel and Claire had been kept busy decorating the second bedroom in preparation of the arrival of their baby. They had decided not to learn what gender the baby was but Claire had inkling that it was a boy.

They regular attended pre-natal classes much to the discomfiture of Daniel who at first found it very strange to go through the exercises and deep breathing that were being taught.

Mark was kept busy organising the re-enactment on behalf of the Sealed Knot Society. There were many administrate task to see to including an accommodation area for those participating who would bring their own caravans, an area for a Civil War period camp site, tents for cafeterias and tourist shops, the Battle site, car parks and portable toilets. Fortunately plans from previous re-enactments were readily available and only required checking out. Mark did contact the various contractors to see if they were still available to supply the various services and if they were, offered them the opportunity to take part.

One problem that did come to light was that word about the King taking part in the re-enactment had leaked out and many of those taking part wanted to be on the Royalist side. It was common practice that members of the Society could choose in which side they wanted to take part as.

As Cromwell's Model Army had outnumbered the Royalist's at the battle of 1645 and for the sake of realism Mark asked for volunteers to act as Roundheads but when that didn't work he had to delegate some of the members as Parliamentarians, but that still left the Parliamentarian side short of men.

However for some it proved to be a godsend. Several of Edward Okey's troop of participants had deserted him to join the Royalists, which left him short of men.
While in the White bull he complained to anyone who would listen. Hopkins was one of those.

"I don't know why they want to take part as Royalists." He complained. "They have no loyalty at all. They have always taken part as Parliamentarians and as part of my ancestor's troops."

"Perhaps I can help you out there." volunteered Hopkins. "A couple of my friends and me have always wanted to take part in a re-enactment. We've seen them on the television, only problem is we don't have any uniforms or equipment."

Okey's face broke into a smile. "That would be great. Yes thanks, I'll get it organised and don't worry about uniforms and that, I'll get some from the previous members of my troop. I can fill you in later on what you would be expected to do at the battle. Don't worry though it's all straight forward. I'll get back to you once I've got things together."

And with that he left Hopkins who was happy with the arrangement. He wasted no time in contacting Jimmy to let him know what Okey had agreed, it was another problem overcome.

After Jimmy had told Ritchie of this good fortune Ritchie sent for Hopkins.

Ritchie handed Hopkins a mobile phone.

"Just as soon as you have been successful with your mission, I want you to phone me immediately and let me know without fail. Do you understand? It's of the utmost importance that I'm notified" he instructed Hopkins.

Hopkins replied that he would do as he was asked and not to worry he wouldn't forget.

Okey had been successful in finding various bits of Roundhead uniforms for the three 'volunteers' but could only muster two muskets. One of them would have to act as a Pike man.
He ran through the drills of loading the muskets with Benjamin and Nathan something they both knew from their previous existence, and what was expected as a Pike man.
During the Civil war it was an honourably profession to be a Pike man and many a gentleman choose to fight this way. Muskets were initially looked upon with some distaste so it was not surprising that Hopkins had chosen to be the Pike man and that fitted in perfectly with their plans.

Okey said that they could travel to Naseby with him and share his caravan while they were there. He left the muskets with them telling them to guard them with their lives as he was responsible for them and it would cause an awful lot of trouble if they were lost. They reassured him that they would be as safe as the Crown Jewels and Okey left to attend to some business. This gave them the opportunity of switching one of the muskets with the modified musket without Okey knowing.

The Battle of Naseby in 1645 took place in the open fields and rolling countryside of Northamptonshire near to the villages of Naseby, Clipson and Sibbertoft. It took place over a large area with an estimated Royalist army of 8,000 facing a Parliamentarian army of 13,500.

Because it was impossible for the Sealed Knot Society to muster such a large number of participants the re-enactment would take place over a smaller select area that could be more easily managed. Mark had conversed with the army and advised them to erect a wire fence around the chosen area that would be the main arena. While the fence alone would not prevent a determined access, small field Radars were positioned at regular intervals. The Radar would pick up any unauthorised movement that would be relayed to the control vehicle and alert the standby section that dressed in Jet Suits could be at the breached section within minutes.

 Members of the public who were attending to view the Battle would be directed through a metal detector gate controlled by armed soldiers who would carry out random checks on any suspicious characters.

Members of the Society would enter through a separate gate away from the public. An armed soldier and a Policeman were on duty here to prevent unauthorised access and to check out the members' entering against a list supplied by the Society.

Edward Okey drove his car into the members' accommodation area and reversed his caravan into the allocated space. Benjamin, Nathan and Hopkins had travelled to the site with him as agreed and helped him with his reversing. They had arrived two days earlier than required for the re-enactment but thought that this would give them all some time to familiarize themselves with the terrain and take part in the practice session before the main Battle enactment the following day. It would also give the three assassins the opportunity to locate and recover the rounds hidden in a Portaloo.

Billy Morrison had sent a text to Jimmy that the items were hidden in a Portaloo for the disabled just as they had agreed. All of the Portaloo's were numbered; the one that they were interested in was number nine. Billy had made several trips to the re-enactment location and unloaded his cargo of Portaloo's in various zones around the area without a hitch, so all that was left now was for Hopkins and his two men to recover the three rounds of ammunition.

On the morning of their first day at the site while Okey was busy discussing with the organisers their part in the next day's battle the three men split up to search the site for the numbered Portaloo. It was Nathan who found Portaloo Number Nine in the main public car parking area and locking himself inside carefully felt around the vent pipe until he found the other plastic tubing. Gently squeezing the tube he felt the shape of the rifle rounds near to the bottom of the tube.

Using his pocketknife he gently cut through the plastic and extracting the rounds placed them into a leather pouch that he had slung at his waist. Returning to find the others he told them that he had the items in his pouch so now everything was set for go.

Mark had been back to Hexham over the weekend prior to the date of the re-enactment to collect his horse and had returned with two extra bodies. He had with much difficulty persuaded Daniel and Alan to take part on the Parliamentarian side. They had both over the last few years helped Mark out by taking part in some of the re-enactments so this would be no different. Daniel however was reluctant to leave Claire because of the forthcoming arrival of their baby.

"I'll be fine." she told Daniel. "Don't worry, junior won't be arriving for a while yet? Besides Dad needs you to drive down with the caravan, otherwise he'll be sleeping under the stars." She laughed.

Mark had transferred ownership of the electric car over to Claire's name after the announcement of only one car per household came into force.

"Only if you're sure." Daniel replied, "I'm not happy about going and leaving you by yourself."

Claire smiled back at him. "If it will stop you worrying I'll go and stay with Kath while you're away. How's that?" she asked.

Realising any further protest would be useless Daniel went to pack some clothes and overnight kit while Claire phoned Kath to organise a few days at her place.

They left Hexham on the Friday, the day before the re-enactment was due to take place. On arrival and after getting the caravan parked and Mark's horse fed and watered they settled down for the evening, except for Mark who went to discuss some points with the organisers.

On his return Mark told the two friends that they were to join Edward Okey's troop of Roundheads the following morning as Pike-men.

Unlike the battle of 1645 that took place beginning in the early morning the re-enactment of 2028 was scheduled to take place in the afternoon. This would allow spectators traveling from any distance time to arrive and not miss any of the action.

After consuming a light lunch on the day of the Battle Daniel and Alan made their way to the Site Management Centre where they drew some suitable Roundhead clothing from a centrally held supply and two Pikes. The Pikes were made from telescopic fibreglass tubing that were more easily transportable and lighter instead of a sixteen feet length pole of an authentic Pike. After dressing in the uniform of their previous enemy they made their way to find Edward Okey's band of men who they were informed were gathered at the Assembly Area.

On their arrival they recognised several of the men and spent some time in conversation with them until Okey appeared and instructed everyone to form two lines, one of Musketeers at the front and Pike men at the rear.

Daniel could not help but notice how three of his fellow Roundheads made sure that they were placed together in line, even roughly pushing away others that came too close to them. Normally members didn't act that way as most of them knew each other or were close friends. Something seemed not quite right. There was something vaguely familiar about them especially the broad shouldered one but he couldn't quite place what it was. He pointed them out to Alan and had that familiar feeling in the stomach before a battle that something was going to happen.

They both found places close to the men who were acting out of place deciding they would watch them and see if their strange behaviour continued.

Okey began briefing the gathered men on what they would do once inside the area and how they were expected to act.

"We will march in and join up with those already there and form two lines facing the Royalist army, Musketeers at the front. We will be quite close to the opposing army because of the limited space in the allocated area. However it is intended that the Musketeers will fire off one volley, reload and fire off another before we close in for the close quarter fighting. Has anyone any questions".

There were none.

"Good. Right turn, forward march." ordered Okey, and the band of men set off for the arena.

Okey marched alongside them, wishing he were on a horse, as his ancestor would have been leading his company of Dragoons to the fight.

As they approached the members' entrance they slowed down and came to a halt. Okey strode forward to find out what the problem was.

A Policeman and a soldier stood at the gate checking each man's name against a list of those carrying a musket before allowing them through the gate. The soldier was inspecting each musket before handing it back to its owner.

Hopkins was not slow to see what was happening. He saw Nathan looking at him for guidance. It would not take long for the soldier to realize that Nathan's musket was different from the others. They were close to the gate now, Benjamin was having his musket checked and was ushered through into the arena. As Nathan was about to have his musket checked Hopkins stepped backwards and brought his foot hard down on the man's toes behind him. The man screamed out in agony.

"You great clumsy Oaf." the man shouted, "What do you think you're doing?"

"What did you call me?" Hopkins cried. "Nobody calls me that and gets away with it." And he punched the man's face knocking him to the ground.
Hopkins jumped astride the man's chest and sitting astride him began to slap his face with an open hand.

"Apologise now or I'll rip your face off." He threatened.

Hopkins victim was now crying out loudly in alarm at his unwarranted assault.

Everyone looked to see what the commotion was about and what was happening. Nobody went to help the unfortunate man on the ground being beaten by Hopkins until the Policeman and the soldier ran over to drag Hopkins off his unfortunate victim.

Nathan and Benjamin quickly exchanged weapons while everyone's attention was focussed on what was happening with the two men on the ground and before the two guardians of the gate returned.

Hopkins glanced over at Nathan who gave a brief affirmative nod of his head. The Policeman was about to have Hopkins arrested for assaulting the other man but Hopkins leant down and helped his victim to his feet. He began apologising while brushing grass and leaves off the man's clothes, saying someone had pushed him and he never intended to hurt the poor man.

Okey intervened saying that the delay would affect the Battle's performance and could they please get on with it. The victim said he didn't want to press charges and that he just wanted to forget about it. Hopkins shook his hand, praising his decision.

The checking of muskets resumed until everyone was through the gate into the arena. Benjamin asked Nathan in a loud voice if he would hold his musket while he adjusted his belt, and once done, retrieved his own musket back from Nathan. Nathan now had the modified rifle back in his hands.

Okey once again ordered them to forward march and then a right wheel bringing them into line with the other Parliamentarian soldiers already there. After halting them he ordered a left turn so that they were facing the Royalist army a short distance away.

Once everyone was in place the order to "Prime and Load Muskets" was given. This was a start of a series of orders to prepare the Muskets for firing with every one doing the set procedure at the same time.

Nathan went through the procedures the same as the rest so that he didn't look out of place. It was only when the order "Mark Ready" was given that Benjamin stepped in front of Nathan so that he could rest his rifle on his shoulder and Nathan fed the 5.56mm round into the rifle's chamber. No one really noticed these unexpected movements except Daniel who was closely watching them and saw what was happening. He saw Nathan load the bullet into the modified musket and realizing what it was dropped his pike and calling for Alan made for the pair of Musketeers.

The order "Fire" was given and the noise of a ragged volley from the muskets covered the sharp crack as Nathan fired the rifle.
The hollow point round travelling at over 2800 feet per second was on its way to the King.

The bullet flew past the King's head and buried itself harmlessly in a bank some distance away. The King had felt the air parting as the bullet flew past his head but hesitated before calling out to his bodyguards that he thought that he had been shot at. They in any case couldn't make out what he was saying because of the noise of the battle.

Nathan realised that he had missed and had quickly reloaded the rifle but in doing so the wax had come off the tip of the round and as the contents of the hollow head spilled out it was caught by the light breeze blowing it back into Nathan's face. Nathan unable to avoid the fine white powder nearly choked as he swallowed some of it but taking careful aim fired again.

In that split second of the round leaving the rifle the King's horse, perhaps startled by the crack, reared its head backwards and took the round just below its eye.
The hollow point exploded on impact, shattering the horse's head killing it instantly. The horse reared backwards and fell onto its

side trapping the King's leg wedged in his stirrup, under its solid weight.

A loud cry was heard from the crowd of watching spectators that the King was down; at the same time a commentator belonging to a broadcasting team from the BBC cried loudly into his microphone that something was wrong and that the King had been thrown to the ground.

Chapter 12

The Battle for Westminster

That morning in London an unusual large number of people some carrying placards with various slogans began arriving at most of the capital's main bus and rail stations.

As part of standard procedures this information was passed up the Metropolitan Police chain of command until it reached the Commissioner of Police who queried what demonstration was scheduled for that day. Checks revealed that no permission had been requested or granted to hold a demonstration and therefore no additional Police had been assigned to control and monitor any demonstration. While the Security Services were aware of the planned demonstration they had not passed this information to the Police fearing that if they did so it might reveal their source and compromise their White Bull operation.

When the crowds began to gather at Park Lane before their march to Parliament Square, a message went out to off duty Policemen to report in for duty while at the same time the Police trainees at the

Metropolitan Police Training Centre at Hendon were also put on standby for crowd control.

Ritchie's plan for the day was simple. Once he had received confirmation from Hopkins of the King's demise he would enter the Palace of Westminster and make a nationwide broadcast from the House of Commons of the news of the King's end and that he was now taking control of the UK in the name of the Republic of Great Britain.

But first he had to get past the Police guarding the entrance to the Palace. He had with Jimmy's help found some members of the organisation who had the training and the experience to take on a key part of his plan to achieve this.

James Ferguson and John Greenhead were both ex Parachute Regiment soldiers who had both volunteered to secure the entrance to Westminster accompanied by Mike Evans who was also an ex-member of the Royal Marines. Their task would be to disarm the Police who controlled the visitors' entrance and ensure that the entrance was kept open for Ritchie and his followers to enter. But to achieve this they would require some guns to be available on the other side of the Visitors Police Checkpoint.

For a number of years restoration work had been taken place to repair the crumbling Palace. The guns would be smuggled into

Westminster by one of the Builders workmen who was also a member of RGB ready for the ex-servicemen to collect.

Two weeks earlier at the Builders depot three 9mm pistols with two full magazines each had been sealed separately into plastic bags and secretly placed inside a Portland cement sack. The cement sack had been carefully resealed and marked with a splash of blue paint. The sack was then added amongst others onto a pallet of cement destined for Westminster Palace.

While all Lorries entering Westminster had their loads checked, one sack of cement amongst many others passed inspection and was unloaded at the builders' compound. Choosing a time that was quiet the RGB workman made a point of restacking the cement onto another pallet until he came to the sack marked with blue paint. Slicing it open with a shovel he recovered the sealed plastic bags and found a temporary hiding place for the guns.

When he had the chance he relocated the guns to the male visitors' toilet near to the visitors shop and placed them into three of the male toilets water cisterns remembering each closet number in sequence from the toilet's entrance door. He then sent a text to Mike Bradley to let him know his items would be delivered in boxes numbered.., and he gave him the closet numbers.

On the Morning of the demonstration the three men, two of them accompanied by women posing as their wives, entered the Palace by the Visitors Gate. Once they were through the Police Checkpoint they made their way to the Visitors Cafeteria and sat at separate tables. One by one the men retrieved the concealed pistols and returned to the cafeteria to await Ritchie's mobile call ordering them to secure the gate.

The crowds in Parliament Square were now a few thousand strong. There was something approaching a carnival atmosphere with a few amateur bands and buskers playing music at various points and the younger members of the crowd dancing and singing with them. Others were waving placards with different slogans and chanting various messages.

It seemed that word of the demonstration had spread far and wide with members of various protesting factions from all parts of the country attending.

Ritchie had gathered around him a hard core of fifty or so street fighters, dressed in a nondescript uniform of black leather jackets, baseball caps and scarves and masks to obscure their faces'. These were his storm troopers, his shock troops, his iron fist who would on his instruction charge and smash through the thin Police line so that he could gain access to the building. Ritchie in turn was waiting for the mobile phone call from Hopkins saying mission accomplished. He kept checking his watch surely they had done the job by now.

One of his companions was idly viewing a news channel on his mobile when a news flash reported that something had happened to the King at a re-enactment battle.

He told Ritchie of the news.

Ritchie tried phoning Hopkins but no answer.

He then decided because of the radio broadcast that Hopkins must have succeeded and sent a text to the waiting group inside Westminster to go ahead and secure the gate and also to the groups waiting at the Royals accommodation to capture their targets.

Gathering his shock troops around him Ritchie told them what he wanted.

"I want to get inside that building and I want you to get me inside. I want to get through that Police line. Will you help me do it?" he asked them.

There was a rousing cry that they would.

"OK. Good, I knew that I could depend on you. Let's go. Make a way through the coppers and get me into the Palace. The doors will be open for us."

Ritchie's shock troops prepared for action. Placards were dismantled so that the wooden shafts were turned into clubs and some with their ends already sharpened to be used as spears. Others amongst the group pulled knuckle-dusters from their pockets and slipped them onto their fists. They were ready.

The Police saw what was happening and closed ranks as the menacing mob of black-jacketed men approached them but with only their truncheons for defence they were soon battling for their lives.

The Police inside the Palace at the visitors' checkpoint saw what was happening outside and sent one of their numbers to close the great iron studded gates that led into the Great Hall. Ritchie's group who were still inside prevented the man from closing the gates and after handcuffing him to the iron railings made their way to the rear of the Police checkpoint.

The Police cordon outside had been breached and the mob was forcing its way through to the visitor's entrance where the Police inside stood ready to repel them. The visitors' gate had been locked and barred much to the frustration of the mob that hurled obscenities at the small band of Police inside and threw stones and sharpened sticks at them through the iron bars of the broken windows.

The Police inside did not notice Ritchie's group until one of the group, James Ferguson, fired a round into the ceiling.

"Open the gate and let them in." He demanded.

The Policemen were startled by the shot but none of them moved to obey. The demand was repeated. Still no one moved.

Ferguson called over the Police sergeant in charge.

"Open the gate." He told him.

"I can't do that." the sergeant calmly replied.

"OK then." Ferguson said and shot the nearest Policeman in the leg who fell screaming to the ground.

"Open the gate." Ferguson repeated. "Otherwise I'll shoot him in the kneecap and then his other leg. Do you want to be responsible for him being a cripple?"

The sergeant knew the injured man and his family as well as he knew all of the others. He couldn't allow him to be crippled.

"OK, OK." He surrendered to Ferguson's demands and ordered one of the other Policemen to open up the gate.

The mob came streaming through administering blows to the surrendered defenders as they passed through onto Cromwell Green where they were directed through the gates into Westminster Hall. The mob was now inside The Palace of Westminster.

Ritchie gathered his troops around him. "Well done all of you. You've done what I asked and here we are. Now the next thing is that the Law is going to be coming through those gates. Are we going to let them?" he asked.

"No." the mob answered.

"Right then close the gates and bar them.' Ritchie ordered. "Split yourselves into two groups. One group to stay here and defend the gate and the other group to go to the end of the hall and take position by those stairs." He said pointing to the far end of the Great Hall. "Your task will be to stop anyone coming into the hall from that end. John I want you to stay here and support this group. James," he spoke to the other ex-Para, "I want you to go with the other group and provide fire support for them at their end of the hall. Mike," he addressed the ex-Marine, "You'll come with me and a few others and provide fire power if required. OK everyone let's move."

Ritchie along with a few chosen men with communication skills and knowledge of radio and Television broadcasting set off to the far end of the hall followed by the second group of fighters. After Ritchie and his group passed through the door at the top of the steps that led into St Stephan's Hall the fighters took up positions on the porch at the top of the wide stone steps securely bolting the door into the hall.

Only minutes after the mob had gained entry into the Palace the sound of sirens indicated the arrival of Police reinforcements. Riot vehicles accompanied by Ambulances all with flashing blue lights, drew up along Abingdon Street spilling out Riot Police dressed in their helmets and body armour and NHS medics carrying their first aid satchels, who immediately began attending to the wounded.

The Police Commander quickly organised the reinforcements into sections and on discovering that the mob had entered into Westminster Hall sent a section after them and another section to gain entry through the members' entrance and trap the mob in a pincer movement.

The first section was unable to gain entrance into the Hall because of the locked gates and awaited further instructions. The second section had made it through St Stephan's Hall but also found they were unable to gain entry into Westminster Hall because of the locked door. They radioed the Force commander with the information and were also told to await further instructions.

The Force Commander had reported to the Commissioner of Police of the situation who had informed him that minimum force was to be used in ejecting the mob from the Palace and that the utmost care was to be taken in ensuring no damage to Westminster Palace or its priceless artworks should occur.

The Force Commander gathered his section leaders together and asked for their ideas on a way forward.

For many years the Special Air Service (SAS) Regiment had kept a Sabre Section at a location in the Capital ready for any immediate call out against a terrorist threat. While this situation did not really define a terrorist threat it was believed that their help and advice would be greatly assist the Police. The SAS Team had arrived at the same time as the Police reinforcements and stood by ready to be called upon if required.

After the Force Commander had conferred with the SAS team leader it was agreed that a controlled explosion would be used to open the door in St Stephan's Hall that led into Westminster Hall.

The SAS team's demolitions expert spoke to one of the Palace's security staff and discovered that the door was secured by three bolts, top, middle and bottom of the door. This was good news, as it would not require as much explosive and therefore less damage as per the Commissioner's Orders. He began to make up three small shaped charges that would blow the bolts on the other side of the door.

The SAS Trooper accompanied by four Policemen made their way stealthily along St Stephan's Hall until they reached the locked door leading into Westminster Hall.

The trooper began super gluing the shaped charges to where the bolts on the other side of the door were located. Three of the Policemen carried hessian sandbags filled with damp sand. Two of them also carried sharpened sticks to be used as props for the sandbags. The fourth man was to provide covering fire if required. The sandbags were positioned against the explosive charges to help direct the force of the explosives and to muffle their sound. The door could be repaired but the stained glass windows along the hall would be more difficult to replace.

Once the Trooper was satisfied that all was ready they retreated a short distance back along the hallway.

He spoke quietly into his radio mike to his Team Leader. "Blue 2 to Blue 1 ready to commence. Over."

"Blue 1 to Blue 2,' Came the reply "Commence."

The Trooper called out loudly "Stand clear of the door." He repeated it again and then pressed the button on his hand held command switch. The bottom charge exploded with a muffled bang, then the middle charge the same and finally the top charge. The door swung inwards to give sight to a panic stricken mob. Some of them had not given heed to the trooper's shouted warning and had received injuries from the flying bolts and fittings.

The four Policemen and the Trooper stood back against the wall donning on their gas masks to allow the section of Riot Police to pass them. One of the Police hurled a tear gas grenade into the mob and waited for it to take effect. The mob retreated back into the hall away from the swirling stinging mist. Some of them were left behind and were quickly handcuffed by the Police.

The gas had not yet affected James Ferguson's eyes. He stood at the bottom of the steps and took aim and fired at the leading Policeman who fell as the bullet entered his leg. The Policeman who had accompanied the Trooper raised his carbine and fired two shots at the gunman. Both rounds from the Policeman's carbine hit James in the upper chest spinning him around as he fell to the ground.

The mob ran to the perceived sanctuary of their comrades at the far end of the hall. The Police spilled down the steps and fired more tear gas into the fleeing mob. Soon the fumes reached the far end of the hall causing more of the mob to cough and seek an escape from the tear gas. The only way to escape the stinging fumes was through the barred gates which they soon opened and staggered out into the waiting Police cordon. After handcuffing the subdued mob the Police made them sit with their backs against the iron railings in Cromwell Green while some first-aid workers were allowed to attend to them, bathing their eyes with water and those with breathing difficulties with oxygen and inhalers.

Ritchie and his team of Technicians had narrowly missed being intercepted by the Police as they had made their way through the central lobby and along the commons corridor to the House of Commons Chamber.

Ritchie and Greenhead entered the Commons Chamber while the Technicians carried on to the Television and Radio Broadcasting control room. Greenhead took up position by the door. His job was to prevent anyone entering the chamber while Richie was giving his speech. Once that was done they would all retire to the relative safety of Westminster Hall where they would be safe with the mob until help from the people arrived.

The Technicians quickly powered up the controls ensuring that the master switch that would override all current broadcasts and allow their broadcast to take precedence was selected. They gave thumbs up to Ritchie who took up position on the Speaker's Chair and took a prepared speech from his inside pocket. He gave thumbs up back to the Control Room and as the TV cameras began to broadcast he began to read his speech.

"Citizens of Great Britain. I am speaking to you today from the seat of Democracy from the Mother of Parliaments here in the Palace of Westminster. You may have heard the news that the King has met with a serious accident and will no longer be able to lead this great country. Those of his descendants in line to take his place no longer wish to do so therefore in order to provide guidance and leadership in these turbulent times, I Richard Fox do hereby declare that I will now be President of these lands and do also declare that as from now they will no longer be known as the United Kingdom but will be known as the Republic of Great Britain.

From now on your voice will be heard in decisions made in this house that affect you. No longer will one person from a privileged family who doesn't have your interests at heart dictate what you have to do.

Those of you in the towns and cities throughout these lands who have been tasked to take control of local councils should proceed to do so. All Police forces will provide assistance to my supporters if requested. Not to do so will witness my greatest displeasure. I call upon all soldiers', sailors and airmen to take to the streets and support those who are tasked with taking back control of our country. Senior members of the armed forces and the Police force should now make their way to Westminster Palace where I will brief them on the tasks I will set before them. I will provide further updates periodically to all citizens. That is all for now."

Everyone who had their Radio or TV switched on heard the broadcast including the London Metropolitan Commissioner of Police. "Get that broadcast switched off, and place that idiot making it under immediate arrest" was the order to her staff. The word went out but because it was a privileged broadcast nothing could be done until one constable suggested closing down the nearest electricity substation to Westminster and hope that because of lack of maintenance since BREXIT the Westminster emergency generator would not kick in.

It didn't and as a result of closing down the electricity substation the whole area came to a standstill as the Underground stopped running and with traffic lights out of commission the grid lock of traffic soon spread to other parts of London ensuring total chaos.

Meanwhile back in Westminster a section of Police had been sent to the Commons Chamber to arrest those responsible for the illegal broadcast. They arrived before Ritchie and the others could return to the great hall and came up against Greenhead threatening them with his automatic pistol. Remembering the order that no damage should be inflicted to the walls or fittings the Police withdrew to await further orders.

They were soon reinforced as more Police went up into the public gallery and began spraying tear gas from aerosol containers into the Commons Chamber. Ritchie screamed at them to stop that he was their new President and not to do this to him. The pair quickly succumbed to the effects of the tear gas and staggered out into the Members Lobby. As a coughing and spluttering Greenhead was first to leave still clutching the semi-automatic pistol he was immediately Tasered by the waiting Police who were not inclined to take any risks. Ritchie was close behind him still shouting that he was their new President and could someone get him some water to wash his eyes. He was led away handcuffed behind the stretcher containing an unconscious Greenhead to join the rest of the mob on Cromwell Green.

Because of the traffic chaos created by shutting down the Electric Sub Station, which was likely to last for the remainder of the day, the Police were unable to transfer their prisoners to secure accommodation. It was therefore decided to secure them in the cellars of the Palace until the following morning when the situation should have improved.

Armed Police led the line of handcuffed prisoners down to the cellars and secured them behind a barred door. They were told that any trouble would result in a canister of opened tear gas joining them inside.

It seemed appropriate that four hundred years after Guy Fawkes had planned to blow up the Palace along with King James that the present offenders against the Crown should be imprisoned in the same cellars where the gunpowder had been stored.

Back in Leicester Jimmy was sat in the White Bull waiting for Ritchie's announcement. He had with him ten of his men from the days of when they marched through the streets and fought with those that opposed them as well as the Police. Their job was to take over the local Council Building and secure it for those that would follow and occupy it. There should be no problems as it was a Saturday and the majority of staff would not be at work only those that took payments would be there. Just to ensure there would be no problems and to intimidate the staff they had armed themselves with knives and knuckledusters and a two of them had revolvers. The Landlord was most pleased to have the extra unexpected visitors on a Saturday and provided some platters of nuts and crisps on the bar to stimulate the men's thirst. The men though had been instructed by Jimmy no excessive drinking and to amuse themselves by watching the horse racing on the television. Suddenly a heated argument broke out between one of Jimmy's men and one of the other regulars over who trained or owned one of the horses that were running. Punches were thrown and the fight spilled out into the street. A passer-by using his mobile phone reported to the police about the disturbance and what was happening.

A young Policeman, not long out of training who was patrolling near to the scene, was told to attend and deal with it. By the time that he arrived the fight was over and the men had returned back inside the pub. The Policeman entered to enquire what was going on and find out if anyone was injured. He didn't realise that he was entering into a situation that was still highly charged with anger from Jimmy's group and the other man's friends, neither who had any respect for the Law. As he entered the Bar the conversation died away and all eyes followed him as he made to the bar. He soon became conscious of the hostility towards him but knew that he was too far in to retire. Reaching the bar where the landlord stood behind he decided to assert his authority.

"We've had reports of a disturbance taken place here." He stated in a loud voice "With several people fighting, can you tell me what's going on?"

The Landlord shook his head, "Nothing going on as far as I know." He replied accompanied by grunts of agreement from the crowded room.

 Turning the Policeman asked the nearest to him the same question. Receiving the same answer he asked one of those who had obviously been fighting by the state of his cut lip and bruised face.

 The man stood up, "Are you deaf or what? He angrily shouted, "Why don't you get yourself out of here before you regret it?"

The Policeman straitened his back in an effort to look taller, "Don't talk to me like that, I'm an officer of the Law and if I ask you a question you'll answer it. Do you understand?"

"Oh I understand alright." He replied and he punched the Policeman in the stomach and then in the face knocking him to the ground.

As the policeman lay on the ground trying to recover his breath he began receiving several kicks from those around him. But before he lost conscious he managed to click on the emergency button of his radio that sent out an emergency signal, 'man down, request assistance'. Jimmy went over and pushed those away who were still kicking at the prone figure and told the Landlord to take the Policeman into the back out of the way.

The emergency call had been received by the Police Headquarters as well as by all of the Police in the area who immediately informed their control that they were on their way to attend. On arriving the first crew there burst through the door startling those inside. One of Jimmy's men drew his revolver and fired, narrowly missing the first Policeman through the door. The Police quickly retired outside and informed their HQ that armed gunmen were inside the premises and that shots had been fired. HQ immediately despatched an Armed Response Unit (ARU) to attend and for those already in attendance to await further instructions.

Jimmy was furious at what had happened he was sure this would mess things up. He took the gun off the man who had fired at the Police and slapped him around the face to vent his own anger more than anything. The man left for the toilet to clean up his face and bloody nose and to get out of the way of Jimmy.

A senior officer arrived at the White Bull at the same time as the ARU; he was to take command of the situation and bring it to a speedily and safe conclusion. After being briefed by the first pair of Policemen on the scene he requested a further ARU to attend. Once that arrived he deployed one unit to the rear of the pub satisfied that he now had it securely cordoned off. Using his car's loudspeaker he called for those inside to surrender their weapons and to leave by the front door one by one and lay down on the ground when instructed.

Inside the pub Jimmy's men were looking at him for guidance while the other regulars were questioning each other on what they should do. Most wanted to comply with the Police instructions and began to file out of the door, soon followed by their friends. Eventually only those who remained were Jimmy and his team.

The Police loudspeaker burst into life again ordering those left inside to come out. Jimmy was desperately thinking what he should do. He couldn't outgun the Police he was sure of that but he must get himself and the team away to fulfil their part of the grand plan. Then he realised that he had hostages that he could use as a bargaining tool, the Policeman and the Landlord and his wife. Why not have the Police drive him and his team to the Council offices? They might be there before Jimmy received the 'Go' from Ritchie, but better to get there early than not getting there at all. In fact while Jimmy was pondering on what to do Ritchie was making his short broadcast from Westminster Palace but no one was paying attention to the Television.

"Bring out the copper." He ordered two of his men.

Using the battered and dazed Policeman as a shield Jimmy opened the Pub door and asked to speak with whoever was in charge.

"What is it that you want?" asked the senior Policeman as he stepped forward, "are you ready to surrender?"

"Don't be stupid." Jimmy sneered, "What I want is a bus to take me and my friends away from here and I don't want anyone following us. Understand?" he added "Otherwise your boy here," he shook the dazed Policeman, "will suffer, do I make myself clear?"

"Perfectly," replied the officer, "but it will take some time to organise things."

"You don't have time." Jimmy stated "Have it here within the hour or there'll be consequences."

The officer got in touch with Police HQ advising them of Jimmy's demands. They replied telling him to stand by.

The Prison Service had recently received a bus for transporting prisoners between prisons, but this was no ordinary bus. It could seat up to twenty four prisoners in a normal seating arrangement and while it had the appearance of an ordinary bus the windows were unbreakable. For their own protection the driver and the guard were enclosed in an air conditioned pod separate from the main compartment and in case of any unrest from the prisoners during the journey a harmless, odourless sleeping gas could be released into the passenger compartment by the driver.
The Police quickly got in touch with Leicester Prison to request a loan of the bus, that was readily granted, and with a Policeman driving it; the bus was soon on its way to the White Bull.

On its arrival it parked near to the pub entrance and while Jimmy held the Policeman with an arm around his neck and a revolver against his head the rest of his team boarded the bus. Not bothering with the Landlord or his wife Jimmy was the last to board dragging the Policeman on with him. The door quietly locked after him. Once aboard he spotted the intercom on the driver's pod and lifting the phone ordered him to get going.

"Where to?" asked the driver.

"Just drive. I'll give you directions later." Jimmy told him.

The driver did as he was ordered and after a while gradually began to release the sleeping gas. When it was obvious that all of his passengers were fast asleep he drove to the Police HQ where a welcoming party of Police unloaded the sleeping passengers onto stretchers and after searching them for weapons deposited them into warm cells.

The London RGB Area Controller, Mike Bradley had tasked two groups to monitor the whereabouts of the Royal family targets. They had taken up their watch position on the Tuesday four nights prior to the date the kidnappings were to take place.

Concealed CCTV cameras strategically placed around the Royal's residences had recorded these groups as soon as they had arrived and continued to monitor them.

One of the RGB watchers wives had become suspicious of her husband coming in at all hours and staying out all night. Was he having an affair she demanded to know? He tried to reassure her it was only because of a job he had been asked to do and it wouldn't be for long. She still wasn't happy with his answers and demanded to know more or she was leaving him.

"Look," he said, "Promise not to repeat what I tell you."

"That depends," she replied.

"Mike has given instructions for us to lift a very important person and we're keeping tabs on him for the time being. It's only until Saturday then I'll be back." He explained.

"Well you had better be." and she left it at that.

The wife was meeting with some of her girlfriends the following night. When during the conversation she was asked about how her husband was getting on it was not long before she let slip that he was carrying out a very important job for the Mike, who they all knew, but it was only until Saturday when it would be over.

The following day one of her girlfriends was talking with some of her friends and she mentioned that she thought her friend's hubby was playing away and that he was going to leave her on Saturday. "You should have heard the cock and bull story he told her about kidnapping someone" She told them.

One of those that were listening to her was an undercover Operator from the Security Services. At the earliest opportunity she reported back to her supervisor what she had heard. This was passed up to the Thames House Operations Room where it was checked along with other information about suspicious groups and loiterers around the Royal's residences. Could this be the important person they meant to kidnap?

Not taking any chances it was decided to move the Royals to Scotland out of any harm's way. They could be better protected there in more secure surroundings. However when told of the possibility of an attempt on their lives they refused to be driven away and decided they would stay and face any threat.

The Security Services then decided to act. In the early hours of Saturday armed Police surrounded and arrested all of those acting suspiciously near to the Royal residences and raided the houses of all of those that had been recorded and identified on the recordings made by the CCTV. When Ritchie sent his text giving the instruction to act no one was available to answer. However the mobile phones recovered from the prisoners tied him in nicely with the planned abductions.

Chapter 13

End Game

Back at the re-enactment Hopkins had seen Daniel and Alan making towards them and drawing his sword took up a fighting stance ready to fight and protect Nathan's back. But as Nathan fired the second time Hopkins had glanced over at the target and seen the horse's head explode and not the King's. Realising that the King must still be alive and that there would not be the time or the possibility of another shot, he decided to finish the job himself. He had to make sure that the King was dead before he called Ritchie with the news.

Tearing off his helmet he threw it at Daniel before running off towards the Royalist line. Daniel stepped to one side to avoid being struck by the helmet but in doing so tripped over one of the lowered Pikes and fell to the ground. By the time he regained his feet Hopkins had a good start but realising that Hopkins intended some mischief Daniel raced after him.

Nathan reached out and grabbed at Daniels tunic as he went past but Daniel turned and pushed Nathan into the group of men behind him sending them all sprawling on the ground. Daniel carried on leaving Alan to deal with Benjamin who had raised his musket to strike at him. Before the musket's butt could strike its target Alan seized the musket and rammed it hard into Benjamin's throat closing his windpipe and cutting off his air. Benjamin fell to the ground gasping for breath as Alan took off after Daniel.

Nathan regained his feet and went over to help Benjamin but as he reached his friend he stared in horror as Benjamin's body began to crumble and fade away into dust. The blow Alan had delivered had been fatal and Benjamin was dead. Nathan turned and ran back through the members' entrance, out into the fields until he came to a small wooded area where he took shelter amongst some bushes. He tried to gather his thoughts on what to do next but became suddenly aware of feeling nauseous and of a burning inside his chest.

Both of the Kings bodyguards dressed as Royalist soldiers were bent over the King trying to free him from the deadweight of the horse. One of them sensed Hopkins arrival and turning made to stand up only to receive Hopkins sword through his shoulder. Before the other kneeling man could draw his concealed pistol Hopkins made a slashing blow and brought the sword down on the bodyguard's helmet, knocking him dazed to the ground,

Daniel caught up with Hopkins as he reached the trapped King. Just as Hopkins raised his sword to deliver a killing blow Daniel leapt on Hopkins back sending them both staggering. The King lay helpless struggling to free his trapped leg as the two men fought over him.

As Hopkins regained his balance he turned to face Daniel, a glimmer of recognition crossed Hopkins face as he remembered the Royalist that he had fought and who had laughed at him all those years ago.

"So you survived the real Naseby Battle and are still with us are you?" he asked Daniel in a sneering voice.
 "But not for much longer methinks." And he lunged at Daniel burying the point of his sword in his neck severing one of his main arteries.

 As Hopkins withdrew the sword Daniel grabbed hold of its blade preventing Hopkins from using the sword against him or the King and held onto it tightly even as the blade cut deeply into his hands.

Alan arrived just too late to save his friend from the sword thrust and as a weakened Daniel fell to the ground he swung his arm and brought the butt of the musket down on Hopkins head crushing his skull with all of the force he could muster.

Daniel had fallen to the ground and lay on his side holding his throat trying to stop the spurting blood as his life drained away. Alan knelt by him trying to help his friend while calling out for help. Daniel reached out and with what strength he had left he pulled Alan's head close to his and whispered to give his love to Claire. Alan drew back startled as Daniel faded away to dust, until nothing of him remained only the clothes that he had been wearing. Alan looked over to where Hopkins had fallen it was the same there only an empty pile of clothing.

Within minutes the Flying Police Team in their Jet Suits and Flying Hoover Boards arrived and cleared the area around the King shunting the crowds away. Other Police and soldiers arrived and together helped to roll and drag the dead horse off the King until his leg was free.

An army ambulance with a doctor and medics came bouncing over the rough ground and drew to a halt near to the King. After a brief examination the King was lifted onto a stretcher and carried to the ambulance where he was safely placed inside. The ambulance left with its blue lights flashing and siren wailing on its way to hospital. An escort of two long wheelbase LandRover's full of armed Police took up positions before and behind the ambulance.

Mark as the event co-ordinator, arrived not long behind the Police and showing his Security Services ID Card he was allowed through the Police cordon. He made straight to where Alan was still crouched alongside the empty clothing where his friend had died and listened to what Alan had to say.
Taking command of the situation he informed the Police Commander who he was and ordered that those close to the scene who had witnessed what had taken place to be detained.

After being checked at the hospital the King gave a broadcast to the nation informing every one of his continued good health after an unfortunate accident at which no one was seriously hurt. He went on to say that he had been told in some places that criminals had attempted to cause trouble in the streets and asked that all loyal citizens should support the forces of law and order.

Fortunately unlike pre BREXIT days the King had reinstated the Police and army to their correct levels of manpower. The Commander of UK Forces issued an order for all servicemen to be confined to barracks and to be put on standby in support of the Police to quell any civil unrest.

The Police themselves had acted quickly and took up station in and at all of the centres of administration in towns and cities. The called for revolt by Ritchie's organisation was slow in getting started and did not develop as Ritchie had wished. There were incidents mainly in the large cities where mobs had gathered and refused to disperse where the army was called in to support the Police. These mainly resulted in tear gas being fired into the crowds and army snatch squads capturing the rabble-rousers and ringleaders. However the broadcast by the King had a calming influence on the nation and the protests soon fizzled out.

Soon after Mark and his colleagues had provided the information from the RGB Treasurer's laptop computer to the MI5 Controller that the surveillance of the names they provided began. This resulted in more people belonging to the RGB organisation becoming known. After the attempted coup the Police made nationwide arrests and while most of the criminals were arrested, one or two did slip through the net.

Mark through his connections helped to hush things up at what had happened at the re-enactment. No crime had been committed for there were no bodies. The two King's bodyguards recovered from their wounds and were retired with a generous pension. Members of the Sealed knot Society who had witnessed the scene were put in quarantine for a short while and made to sign the Official Secrets Act before being told what they had witnessed was a security exercise. The King's horse was reported to have been startled by the musket fire causing the King to fall off. No explanation of the horse's exploding head was given.

It was a downcast Mark and Alan that returned to Hexham neither of them looking forward to telling Claire of Daniel's loss.

Claire saw the vehicles pull into the drive and went out to meet them. She was surprised that only Mark and Alan got out of the cars.

"Where's Daniel?" she asked with some rising concern showing in her voice.

"Let's go inside." Her father answered. "I'll explain things to you there." He preferred her to be sitting down when he broke the news.

Once inside with Claire seated on one of the straight-backed chairs Mark gently began to tell her. "I'm very sorry Claire but Daniel won't be coming back. He died during the re-enactment while preventing an assassin from murdering the King. He gave his life in order to protect him."

Claire looked at her father not believing at first at what he had said and then the words penetrated her shocked mind.

"Where is he?" Claire asked "I want to see him, where is he?" she asked again.

Mark looked across at Alan before answering her. "I'm afraid that's not possible." He told her. "It seems that Daniel's body is not here. It just faded away, turned to dust. Alan will tell you, he was with Daniel when it happened."

"That's right Claire" Alan broke in "Daniel was stabbed by one of the men that followed us through the Worm Hole when we first arrived. I was just too late to prevent it from happening and was with him when he died. If only I'd been a few seconds quicker. I might have saved him. I just can't forgive myself"

"Don't blame yourself Alan." Claire replied, "I'm sure that you tried your best. Tell me" she asked, "What happened to the person who stabbed him?"

"He died as well. I saw to that but not so brave or as honourable as Daniel." Alan told her.

"There is something else Claire." Alan continued, "His last words to me were 'give Claire my love'. You were in his thoughts at his last moments."
The shock that her father was afraid would hit her had not yet taken effect and she asked, "Why Oh why did this have to happen. We were so happy. Everything was going so well. And why did his body turn to dust?"

"I suppose." her father answered, "It was because this was not his time he was not meant to be here but he can live on in his son." he added.

Alan looked at them both "Merkle told us that everything has a purpose. He said there must be a reason why we arrived at Camelot when we did. I think that reason must have been to send us here and prevent the King from being murdered, and perhaps for the two of you to meet each other."

Everyone in the family was shocked by the news of Daniel's death as were all of the friends that he had made and the workers at the business workshop.

There had to be a funeral so that the true facts would not become known. Daniel had to have a proper burial and the casket had to contain a body otherwise the undertakers and crematorium staff would ask questions about an empty coffin. Mark's colleagues in the Security Services prepared a sealed casket containing the body of one of the many unidentified bodies that are stored in mortuaries around the country, waiting to be claimed by a relative who never appears. At least one of these poor souls would have a proper burial. The Police escorted the casket to Hexham where a quiet funeral at the crematorium took place, attended by family and friends.

The local newspaper contained a brief message in the Births and Deaths section that due to a sudden illness brought on by Sepsis Daniel Colbert passed away at his home in Hexham.

Part 3
Chapter 14

Home Coming

Daniel came to lying naked on a cold stone floor, the rough slabs pressed against his cheek. Gradually regaining his senses he turned his head slightly and opening his eyes he began to focus on his surroundings. Slowly he realised that he was in the underground room in the castle and lifting his head he saw Merlin sitting at the bench looking at him. It all came flooding back to him. Daniel remembered what had happened and reached up to his throat. There was no wound and no blood.

Merlin bent over him and spoke in a quiet voice. "So you are back with us then. Don't worry," he reassured Daniel, "Your wound is healed, and there is no blood. You will be fine. Here cover yourself with this," he said throwing Daniel a rough woollen cloak, "until we can find you some clothes"

Wrapping the cloak around his shoulders Daniel sat up confused hardly daring to believe that he was alive.

"How did I get here? He asked, "And where is Alan? Is he with me?"

Merlin paused before answering. "I am to tell you that Alan is not here with you and that you travelled alone. The power that rules this universe, the power that put us here has decided that you will not be lost in the mists of time so you have been returned to the beginning of your brief journey. The memories that you have will soon fade and what you have experienced will only be remembered as a dream." He offered Daniel his hand and with surprising strength lifted him to his feet.

"You're a good man Daniel that is why you have been returned here. Those that are evil or have evil intent and are beyond redemption would forever be lost in the mists unless the ancients have further use of them. You are to return to your family and live out your life in peace. You still have much to achieve and may be called upon again when the time is right. When the people ask of Alan say that you became separated at Naseby and that you have not seen him since. He will be remembered as one of the thousands that were lost in the English Civil War. But come," Merlin motioned that Daniel should follow him, "you must be hungry, let us go and dine before you leave here."

Outside the castle and further along the beach three naked riders rode furiously after the soldiers who had just left the castle. Captain Jeremiah Hopkins and his two soldiers Benjamin Castle and Nathan Levin found themselves riding hard to catch up with the others. None of the three could remember anything and had no idea why they were sat naked on their horses galloping along the beach; the last thing that they remembered was entering the beach looking for Royalists.

Overtaking the soldiers Jeremiah brought them to a halt, the smirks and laughter from the soldiers aimed at the three men soon died away as Hopkins glowered at them and ordered them to pass them their spare clothing. None of the soldiers dared question him about his absence or what he and the others had been doing or what they had done with their clothes for fear of punishment. Suitably attired once again Hopkins took the lead and directed the troops back to the main Parliamentarian Army camp.

After returning to the camp and finding replacement clothes and armour from the stores waggon Jeremiah was ordered to report to Lord Fairfax for fresh orders. He was told to take his troop to Carlisle where the Scottish Covenanters army were laying siege to the town and castle. It was thought that if troops of Cromwell's army were to be seen arriving in support of the Scots, then it might influence the defenders to surrender more quickly. Once the castle had been taken he was then to report to the Senior Commander at Newcastle and provide support for the garrison of Scottish Covenanters soldiers who were occupying the town after its recent surrender.

It was early the next morning that Merlin awakened Daniel from a deep sleep.

"Your horse is saddled and some provisions have been provided towards your journey." He told him. "They will not last you for very long but will help you on your way." He also handed him a sword and a dagger, adding that he thought he may have use for them on his way home.

Reaching for a wooden bucket Daniel hurriedly threw some of the cold water over his face and quickly pulled on the clothes that Merlin had provided.

They both made their way to the stables where Daniel's horse stood patiently waiting; but there was no sign of Alan's horse. Daniel reached for his cloak that was still slightly damp from the previous day's rain. He was beginning to doubt what his brain was telling him that this was all unreal. But where was Alan if that was the case.

Turning to Merlin Daniel said "Merlin I feel at times that I am losing my mind. Sometimes things are so real and at others it's as if it's all a dream."

"Remember what I said." Merlin replied, "Your thoughts and memories of what has gone before will eventually fade and you will remember none of it. Now be gone you have a long journey in front of you. It has been good to meet you Daniel. I have a feeling that we may well meet again."

Mounting his horse and bidding goodbye to Merlin Daniel rode across the wooden bridge on the start of his journey home.

It took several weeks before Daniel reached Hexham after encountering numerous incidents along the way. Once the provisions that Merlin had supplied were gone he took to laying snares while he slept overnight in hedgerows. There was an abundance of Rabbits, which he was regularly successful in catching.

He began to think less and less about his recent past as his memory slipped away and concentrated on staying safe in what was for him, a dangerous land.

At night when he slept he had restless dreams of big silver birds in the sky that devoured many people at once and roared as they flew overhead and of metal boxes that transported people to their destinations. In one particular reoccurring dream he saw the face of a girl who spoke to him but the face was always a little out of focus and he couldn't quite make out what she was saying, and then when he reached out to her she faded away.

He did his best to avoid contact with any others that came his way in case they were Parliamentarian sympathisers. It was only at remote farms when his horse needed rest and fresh hay that he asked for food and shelter. He paid for any kindness with a day's work helping out around the farm in any way that he could.

On one occasion his horse lost a shoe and he was forced to enter a village to seek out the blacksmith where he drew curious glances from the villagers some of whom wanted to know his business. Paying the blacksmith out of his small amount of monies he was on his way as quickly as possible. But he had drawn the attention of two men who decided to follow him.

After putting a fair distance between himself and the village he found a good spot to bed down for the night. Unsaddling his horse and tethering it to a tree Daniel set up some snares, wrapped himself in his cloak and curled up under a bush. Not long after the sun had gone down and darkness had fallen Daniel was woken by the sound of his horse grunting. Easing himself quietly from his bed he could see silhouetted against the sky someone trying to unfasten the horse's tether. Unsheathing his sword he quietly made over to the horse.

"What are you think you're up to." He cried out, confronting the dark figure of a 'would be' thief.

The startled thief turned at Daniel and swung at him with a weighted club. Daniel ducked and as it swung past his head, he drove his sword into the assailant's armpit. The man cried out and dropping his cudgel ran off. Daniel sensing that someone was behind him swung around with his sword held at shoulder height. The edge of the sword found a second man and sliced through his cheek and nose. The man fell backwards to the ground dropping a long bladed knife as he fell. Daniel stepped over him and held the point of the sword to the man's throat.

"Tell me why I shouldn't lean on this a little harder?" he asked.

The grounded assailant begged for mercy saying his family would starve if he didn't return.

Daniel hesitated before replying making the second thief sweat a little.

"Unfasten your belt and stand up." He ordered his assailant. He knew the man would be no further threat while holding up his trousers. "Now be gone and tell your friend and any others they will not be as fortunate as yourselves if they return."
The man rolled to his feet holding his torn face and clutching the waistband of his trousers staggered away.

Daniel picked up the discarded belt and dagger placing it into its sheath and slinging the belt around his shoulder quickly saddled his horse. Finally gathering up his snares along with one captured rabbit, he left the scene of the attempted robbery to find a new place to bed for the night. He did not want to be here if the men returned with more of their friends.

The following morning Daniel continued on his journey north. The northern part of England had always been a strong supporter of the King but after the Battle of Naseby and with little or no opposition from the Royalists army the Parliamentarian forces had begun to exert their control. The further north that he travelled the more he came across burnt out farms where perhaps the inhabitants had given shelter to Royalist soldiers and had paid the ultimate price.

He began to worry what he would find when he reached Hexham and how his family had fared.

He gave York a wide berth knowing that it had fallen to the Parliamentarian forces and cut across country through the Dales and Fells until eventually arriving on the outskirts of Hexham. He took his time in observing the area especially for any sign of Roundheads. When he was quite satisfied that no enemy soldiers were in the town he made his way to his house.

He let out a sigh of relief to find it still standing and free from any damage. Townsfolk stopped and stared at this stranger but some began to realize who he was and excitedly began to tell their neighbours.

Daniel dismounted from his horse and tethered it to a ring set in the wall of the house just as the door opened and Denise stepped out followed by two small children.

For a few brief moments they stared at each other taking in the change of three years of separation and then they were in each other's arms.

"Welcome home husband" she smiled at him "We have missed you it seems so very, very long ago that you left and we have a new addition for you to meet."

She reached down to the small child hiding behind his mother's skirts and lifted him up.
"Thomas this is your father." And she placed him into Daniels arms.
The boy buried his face into Daniel's shoulder trying to hide his shyness.

"I didn't know when I left that you were expecting a child. You never said." Daniel answered.

"I didn't want you to go away worrying about me or the birthing. Anyway all went well as you can see."

Daniel leant down and scooped up his daughter.

"What a big girl you've grown into." He told her, and she planted a big kiss on his cheek.

"Where's my father?" Daniel asked his wife.

Denise evaded the question. "Come inside," she told him "You must be hungry after your journey."

They entered the house into a large room that served as a dining area, and a workshop where the family business was run from. A cooking area with an open fire was at the rear and some stairs led up to two bedrooms in the floor above.

"Where's my father?" Daniel asked again.

"He's not here," Denise, replied, "I'm sorry Daniel. He died two weeks ago."

Daniel was quiet as he took in the news. "What was it, was it the plague?" he asked, "I heard that there is an epidemic and many people are dying."

"It wasn't the plague." His wife replied. "There was a troop of Roundheads staying here overnight. They were on their way from Carlisle to reinforce the garrison at Newcastle. We were ordered to give shelter for three of them. They were well mannered at first but that evening after they returned from the Tavern they sent me for more Ale. When I returned they began to molest me. Your father heard my cries and made to protect me. The three of them set about him and beat him very badly. He never recovered from the beating and died from his injuries."

"And what happened, did they succeed in molesting you?" he asked. Not wanting to say the word what he really meant.
"They beat me as well." She replied. "Especially the big one he enjoyed hurting me. He bit me so hard I couldn't help but cry out. That's when your father arrived and tried to stop them."
"And did they succeed in molesting you?" he asked again

Denise was quiet, she knew what he meant. She did not want to tell the truth because she knew it would hurt him but he would eventually find out by the village gossip.

"Yes, they held me down and took their turns with me." She began to sob remembering the helplessness of that night.

"And where were the children?" Daniel asked.

"They were upstairs in their bed. The soldiers didn't bother them. I think they forgot they were there."

Daniel looked at his wife and felt the guilt inside him that he had not been here to protect her from what had happened or his father from what must have been a one sided fight. If he had hurried more and not stopped at farms to rest on his journey he might have been here to prevent what had happened. Guilt lay deep in his mind.

That night sleep did not come to Daniel as he lay in bed with his back to his wife. He felt the warmness of her against him and his thoughts turned to what she had suffered at the hands of the three soldiers. His mind was in turmoil, so many thoughts. What can he do what should he do what if his wife was pregnant by the Roundheads? Could he raise such a child as his own? The bitterness and anger inside him grew until at last he rose from the bed and went outside where he wept at what had taken place while he was away.

The next morning Daniel visited his father's grave and sat there silently for a while, staring at the mound of earth that was already sprouting grass and asking his father for forgiveness for not being there when he was needed most. He also swore on his father's grave that the men responsible would pay for their crimes no matter how long it took him to find them.

He next went to the blacksmiths to ask of news of his friend. Alan's father, Andrew, was busy in the forge pumping the bellows to bring the furnace up to its full heat. Welcoming Daniel he left the forge and took Daniel into the house where he asked about his son, as he had not heard anything from him since he left. Daniel was disappointed that there was no news of his friend and began to tell Alan's father of their exploits.

He told him about the Battle of Naseby and how they fled the field with Roundheads in pursuit and that they had become separated during the chase.

His memory, as Merlin had forecast, was gone from his head, nothing of the journey in time or Merlin and the castle remained.

Andrew gave his condolences to Daniel saying, "What bad times they were living in and things must get better." He didn't mention that the entire village knew what had taken place on that night in case Daniel wasn't yet aware.

But Daniel was aware and had thoughts on what must be done. He noticed an old crossbow hanging on the wall and asked if it was for sale. Andrew guessed what was in Daniel's thoughts and said he could have it and that he would make some new bolts for it so that he could do some target practice.

Back at the house Daniel joined Denise who had boiled some hen's eggs and baked fresh bread for the family's morning meal.

Daniel asked his wife if she knew the names of the three soldiers who had stayed at the house.

"I only heard them call each other by their first names. Let me think. One was called Nathan and another Benjamin but they only addressed the big man as Captain but I'm sure I heard the two talking about him to each other and calling him Jeremiah, yes I'm sure that was what the others called him." She shuddered at the thought of them. "Why do you ask?" She guessed what was in his mind. "There's nothing that you can do. They'll be long gone by now."

But Daniel didn't think so and he really didn't care. He would find them no matter where they may be or how long it took and make them rue the day that they came to Hexham. He spent the rest of that week repairing the crossbow with fresh sinew for the string and a further week practising with the new bolts that Alan's father had supplied until he was happy with his accuracy.

Daniel said goodbye to his wife and the children and set off for Newcastle armed with the crossbow in addition to the flintlock pistol tucked in his belt and a new sword and dagger of excellent quality that Alan's father had insisted he take.

It was a melancholy journey as he made his way to Newcastle. His mind was full of thoughts of Alan as he travelled along the well-trodden track that they had taken many times together before they had left to join the King's army.

He tried to blot out the other thoughts of the Roundheads abusing his wife as they only fuelled the anger inside him and he wanted to be able to think clearly when he arrived at his destination.

Chapter 15

Keelmen

Daniel arrived at the eastern end of Newcastle just outside of the town walls and after finding a stable that would look after his horse he walked down to the riverside.

Making his way along a well-trodden footpath he passed rows of Keelboats moored along the shoreline, ready for the next day's work. These boats were forty feet long and nearly twenty feet across but what made them so useful on the river was their shallow draught of less than five feet. This enabled them to navigate the shallow water and sandbanks of the river carrying a cargo of some twenty tons of coal to the waiting sea going colliers at the mouth of the river.

The crews of these boats, known as Keelmen, did not own them but worked them for their owners and received a share of the fee per load for each trip that they made from the coal chutes to the ship. The work was dependant on many factors including the availability of coal. Sometimes the owners of the pits would withhold production in order to inflate the market price or the miners themselves might be on strike. The costal ships, the colliers that transported the coal were dependent on reasonable weather for their journey north from the southern ports where coal was in great demand. During the winter months many ships would not risk this journey or would not enter the mouth of the river because of the many sandbanks and the treacherous *'Black Midden'* rocks resulting in no wages for the Keelmen or food for their families. Many of the Keelmen were forced to find alternative employment if it was available or spend long periods living on credit.

Daniel soon came to the Sandgate area with its many closely built dwelling houses in a maze of twisting alleyways'.

The Sandgate was an area just off the Quayside where the Keelmen and their families lived. The Keelmen were well known for their reputation of hard drinking, hard living men that risked their lives daily supplying coal to the bigger ships. After their working day they would gather at the Quayside drinking dens and slake their thirst.
It was here that Daniel went looking for an acquaintance that he had made during one of his visits with Alan.

While on one of their business trips in previous years, Daniel and Alan had been enjoying a drink of Ale in one of the Quayside

Taverns when they were invited by a group of Keelmen to join them in one of their drinking sessions. Everyone was in good spirits having just been paid their wages. Singing and dancing were the order of the day along with laughter and free flowing drink until a coarse remark from one of the sea going seamen about the Keelmen started a fight.

One of the sailors pulled a knife and was about to plunge it into the back of an older Keelman when Alan grabbed the sailors arm and after removing the knife from his hand picked him up and threw him across the floor. After the rumpus had cooled down and everyone was drinking again the Keelman that Alan had saved from the knife, along with two others came over and introduced himself to the two friends.

"I believe that I owe you my thanks for what you did; it saved me from a great injury if not worse. These sea going lot," he said pointing at the sailors "can't hold their drink. It's always the same when they come ashore two or three Ales and they want to take on the world. My names James McDade, skipper of the best Keelboat on the Tyne." He smiled and held out his hand. "And these two vagabonds, "he pointed at the other two men, "are my crew Billy Johnson and Mattie Robson."

The two Keelmen nodded their greetings to the two friends.

191

"If you're ever in need of help or a place to stay when you're in Newcastle just come and see me and we'll sort things out for you. Just ask for me along at Sandgate, folk will tell you where I am."

Daniel remembered that night and was now on his way to ask the Keelman for his help. After asking several people if they knew where James McDade lived he was finally given directions by someone who knew James. He attracted looks of suspicion as he navigated his way through the maze of alleys for not many outsiders ventured into the Sandgate where the Keelmen ruled.

Arriving at what he guessed was his destination he knocked on the door. An attractive girl in her mid-twenties opened it; her light brown hair cascading over her shoulders outlined a smiling face. She wore a dark green dress that reached just above her ankles and a white pinafore that circled her waist that was intended to keep her dress clean.

"Yes what is it?" she asked.

Daniel's heart skipped a beat. He was speechless while he stared at the girl. The girls face, he was sure it was the same as the one in his recurring dreams.

"Well what is it? She asked again a bit impatiently this time.
"Sorry," Daniel stuttered, "I'm looking for James McDade."
Daniel replied.
"What do you want of him?" The girl asked.

A man's voice from inside called out from inside "Who is it
Charlie, what do they want?"
"Someone looking for you father." she answered

James McDade appeared in the doorway accompanied by a small
black and white dog at his heels that growled menacingly at
Daniel. Even in the dim light given off from the inside lantern
James recognized Daniel straight away.

"Well if it isn't one of the lads from Hexham. Come in, come in."
he bade Daniel to enter. "Charlie," he spoke to the girl, "Get some
Ale for our visitor, there's a good lass. What brings you down this
way? And where's your friend Alan?" he asked Daniel.
The dog sniffed at Daniel as he entered the room.

"Don't mind Sam he won't bite," said James, "Sam's the best Rat
catcher in Sandgate, aren't you Sam?" The dog wagged its tail
hearing its name mentioned or it understood the praise it was
receiving. "We don't get many vermin around here Sam sees to

that." James patted the dog's head before the two men drew up chairs and sat down at a rough table in the centre of the room. Satisfied it would receive no more attention the dog settled down underneath the table.

"Now lad what is it?" the Keelman asked.
"I've come to seek your help." Replied Daniel and he went on to explain what had happened in Hexham.

"I was hoping that you could help me to find these three men, if they are still in Newcastle that is, or if they have left. I need to make them pay for what they've done. I have no faith in the Sheriff, as he'll be under the influence of the military and the Parliamentarians so I don't think I'll get any justice there. Doing it my way they'll get their just deserts according to my law."

"Aye and I can guess what that will be." James smiled. "Of course I'll help you. Us Keelmen have our own way of dealing with the likes of them. Should you need our assistance at any time all you have to do is ask. Anyway it shouldn't be too difficult to find them. I'll put the word around."

James's daughter returned with a flagon of Ale and two wooden cups. Placing them on the table she left them to talk while she carried on preparing the meal she had been busy with before Daniel had arrived.

"I didn't realise that you were married James." Daniel said looking around for any trace of the wife.

"I was but the wife's been gone these last nine or ten years now. It was the plague that took her. It arrived here off one of those foreign ships they say. The wife's mother took ill with it first so the wife went to look after her and then she came down with it as well. The plague took both of them." His voice faltered as he looked towards his daughter. "Charlie here," he nodded his head towards his daughter, "wanted to go and nurse them both but I said no otherwise it might have taken her also."

"I'm sorry to hear that James." replied Daniel. "But you did right not to let Charlie go. The plague doesn't take prisoners."
To change the subject Daniel asked, "If you don't mind me asking, why do you call your daughter Charlie?"
James smiled before replying. "Charlotte was her mother's name so that's what we called her, but don't let her hear you calling her that or you won't be very popular. We also gave her Claire as her middle name after my mother. Charlie's always been something of a Tomboy so we got in the habit of calling her Charlie, which she

prefers than being called Charlotte. Comes out on the boat with me and the lads and can shovel coal with the best of them. But when she's ashore she looks after me and keeps the house all tidy and dresses like the young lady that she is. She's a good girl. I just hope that one of these days she'll find the right man and settle down. Until then she's learning all about the boat and the ways of the River."

Charlie told them that the food was ready and placed a fresh loaf of bread on the table before bringing them each a bowl filled to the brim with a thick stew of meat and vegetables. Bringing a bowl for herself she gave them each a wooden spoon before sitting down at the table with them.

During the meal it was agreed that Daniel would stay with them during his time in Newcastle. He would be safe here in the Sandgate with the Keelmen.

After the meal Charlie made up a bed for him in one corner of the room and rigged a curtain around it to give him some privacy. As Daniel unpacked his valise Sam the dog, tail wagging, sniffed around its contents enjoying the new smells.

The following day true to his word James put the word out to the many Keelmen to find the three named Roundheads who had recently arrived in the town from Carlisle. The Keelmen in turn passed word to the Landlords of the Taverns in the town to look out for any soldiers meeting their description.

It was early morning and another working day as James and his daughter prepared to leave for the Keelboat. Daniel hardly recognized Charlie for she was transformed into what could be mistaken for a young boy. Her hair was tied up under a blue bonnet and she was wearing a linen jacket and knee length breeches similar to her father's attire.

Daniel greeted the pair with a joyful "Good Morning." Which James replied to, Charlie however stared at Daniel with a look that said, 'Dare to make a comment'. Daniel with a smile on his face looked away and said nothing.

After they had left Daniel walked down and along to the Quayside where some sailing boats were moored alongside the jetty busy loading stores, cargo and animals. He entered through one of the gates in the town wall and climbed up a set of steep stairs that brought him up near to the Castle Keep.

His plan was to familiarize himself with the narrow streets and alleyways of the town. He also planned to take special interest in the town walls for it was here that soldiers would be posted as guards to patrol between the many towers. He might at least learn where the Scottish soldiers were billeted and where the Roundheads would be. From there he would look to see where the nearest Taverns would be where the soldiers would eat and drink. He took his time in walking around the two miles of the wall spending most of the day observing where the guards were positioned.

Newcastle town wall was an impressive structure standing some twenty-five feet high and several feet thick with seventeen towers and seven main gates. It had provided protection for the townsfolk many times from marauding Scottish armies over the years; however the mighty walls could not stand up to the power of gunpowder. The Scots had mined the wall and taken the town after several months of siege in October of the previous year. Now they occupied it on behalf of and in agreement with their Parliamentary allies.

While waiting for word from the network of Keelmen regarding the three Roundheads and in between his reconnoitres of the town, Daniel had returned to Hexham several times to visit his family and to see if Alan had returned. It was during one of his visits that Denise told him that she was pregnant and it must be his from when he last returned. Daniel didn't think so he believed that the child was the result of her ordeal by the three Roundheads and while he didn't voice his opinion to Denise, the bitterness inside him grew.

As the seasons began to change and the weather worsened it was not always possible to make the journey to Hexham but he travelled when he could to make sure that his wife was coping with her pregnancy and that the children were in good health. Denise told him not to worry about them as her sister, Alice, was being a great help to her as well as looking after the children so that she could rest. She told him to return to Newcastle and continue with his search. She would send for him if she needed to. As much as he enjoyed being with his family Daniel couldn't put Charlie out of his mind and was looking forward to being with her again.

Back in Newcastle Daniel had settled in to a new way of life living with James and his daughter. He would help out with household duties, fetching fresh water, finding fuel for the fire and by using his skill at catching Rabbits would supplement their diet with a Rabbit stew. On Sundays he would saddle up his horse and with Charlie holding on behind him, and Sam the dog running alongside, they would leave the town for the countryside where they could enjoy the peace and quietness that it offered.

On one of these trips Charlie asked him why he was so determined to find the men he was searching for. She hadn't listened to the conversation between Daniel and her father when he had first arrived and had just accepted that Daniel was staying with them because he was as a friend of her fathers.

"What is it you want of these men?" she asked "do they owe you money or something?"

Daniel told her all what had happened and that he intended to make the men suffer for what they had done.

"I can understand how you must feel," She replied "but why don't you take your grievance to the town's Sheriff, he will see that you get justice."

"I don't believe for one moment that three of Cromwell's men would be found guilty and pay for their crimes. My way justice will be done. I hope that you can see it my way, but if not I'll not put you in a difficult position and I can seek other accommodation."
"You will do no such thing; you are our guest and will remain so for as long as you wish. Besides," she added teasingly "It's nice to have some help around the house."

What she really meant was that she would miss him if he left just the same as she did when he went to visit his wife in Hexham.

During the week Daniel sometimes accompanied the crew of the Keelboat out onto the river and helped them with their work.
The day began with the boat being positioned under the coal chutes where men would shovel the coal from waggons into the chutes so it fell directly into the boat. It had to be spread evenly in the hold so that they could get a full load and keep an even trim. Care had to be taken not to be under the chute when the coal was falling otherwise you could end up with serious injuries. He found shovelling the coal from the Keelboat onto the colliers' back breaking work and marvelled at Charlie who along with the two men had at times to shovel the coal some eight feet up onto the Collier's deck. At the end of the day the men would take a quick dip in the river to clean themselves of the coal dust that had gathered on the sweat of their bodies. James had rigged up a screen on the rear of the boat so that Charlie could attend to her ablutions and douse herself with buckets of water while retaining her modesty from any unwanted stares and return home as clean as when she had left.

He also admired the way that James as the Skipper, once the boat was loaded, would negotiate his way along the river to the larger colliers in deeper water. Moving downstream he was continually changing direction to avoid sandbanks and shallow water only using the large oar at the rear of the boat to steer with while the two crewmen propelled it along with an oar at either side.

"How do you remember when to change direction?" He asked James.

"Comes with experience." James replied. "You get to know the river and where the sandbanks are and when to steer clear. We have a name for some of them. Over there," he pointed to his left, "is 'Shifting Sam' it's always moving depending on the tide, and over there is 'Hidden Hilda', that's there most of the time but you can't see it until you're on top of it. Caught many a skipper out has that. Only way off is to lighten the cargo and push yourself free, and that cost's you time and time is money." They sailed on past the concealed sandbank.

"There's another one over there." He continued pointing towards the south bank. "We call that one 'Journey's End'"

"Why is that?" asked Daniel.

"Remember I told you that us Keelmen have our own way of dealing with those that transgress against us? See those four posts just clear of the water? That's where they end up at low tide, spread-eagled or pegged out on those posts waiting for the tide to come in and pay them what they are due. You must have heard the expression 'pegged out'. Well that's where the saying comes from meaning you're finished or you're at journey's end."

Daniel shaded his eyes to get a better look. He could see the tops of four posts set out in a square about six feet apart with the water lapping against them. He looked closer and was sure that he could make out an arm just clear of the water waving at him.

"There's someone there." He shouted excitedly. "Someone's waving."

"Nay lad." Answered James "There's no one there now, just what's left of him. It's the water moving that's making him wave like that. The rats must have chewed through one of the ropes. Give it another week or two and there'll be nothing left. The tide will have taken it all away. Just in case you're wondering that was a foreign sailor who thought our women were easy. You don't beat and rape a Keelman's woman without paying the price. There was only one foreign ship tied up at the time and we asked its Captain to give us the offender. When he refused we blocked him in with some of our Keels and threatened to set fire to his ship. He saw sense and gave us the one we were after. The lass he had offended identified him and the elders gave him a fair trial before we pegged him out, he got what he deserved."

Daniel starred at the sandbank until it slipped out of sight behind them, his mind formulating a plan.

Daniel was beginning to think that his quarry had left Newcastle. There had been several reports' about three soldiers who fitted the description but after checking those out they proved false.

It was near to the end of the month before word arrived that one of the Keelmen had been told that the men he was looking for might be found at 'Mucky Micks' a drinking den used mostly by soldiers, near to the market area of the town.

It was late one afternoon that Daniel and James set off once again to see if these were the men he was seeking.
James told Daniel that Mucky Micks was a place where the soldiers would go to pick up women from the town. Most of the women who went there had been widowed when their husbands had been killed the previous year defending the town against the

Scottish army. The victors had disbanded Newcastle Corporation leaving no one to provide help for the sick or the poor or the needy. With children's mouths to feed and no means of support, the women had resorted to the only other way of feeding their families that they knew.

Mucky Micks had derived its name from the big Irishman who owned it and like the name suggests, rarely took time to bathe. The building had originally been a cow shed near to the Market but had been burned down during the previous year's fighting. The Irishman had seen the potential in a place where the occupying soldiers could relax and had purchased it. After replacing the roof and making a few repairs he had opened for business and paid some women to frequent it. Word soon got around the soldiers that 'Mick's was the place' and it became very popular with them.

The two men entered the dimly lit room that was thick with smoke from the long pipes that some of the occupants smoked. At the far end of the room were several kegs of Ale mounted on their side across a stout wooden frame. Dotted about the room were rough wooden tables around which sat men with some women on their knees. It was noisy with drunken laughter from the men and false shrieks from the women if the men's hands went somewhere where they shouldn't.

Careful not to trip over the unevenly laid flagstones the pair made their way over to the where the owner stood behind the kegs of Ale observing his customers.

"Hello Mick. How are you?" James greeted the big Irishman.

"Fine sir, fine, and what can I get for you two gentlemen?" the Irishman answered.

"Two tankards of your best Ale and not the horse's piss that you sell to this lot," James pointed at the others around the room, "and we'll have some information to follow." James replied.

"And what information would that be?" Mick replied enquiringly.

"The same information that you gave to my fellow Keelman about three soldiers." Answered James.

The Irishman's mind was sharp and he remembered immediately what it was he was asking for.

"And is there a reward for this information? He asked.

"Of course there is," replied James smiling, "we won't burn this place down and you with it. Now what do you know." He added threateningly.

The Irishman had been in Newcastle long enough to know that the Keelmen were men of their word and wouldn't take kindly to being messed with.

"I was told to look out for three men, soldiers that is, who like to hurt the women. Well the girls here told me about these three and how they enjoy making them cry. The girls don't want to go with them but it's the only way for some of them to earn a penny or two. The men aren't here just now, it's a bit early for them but if you take a seat I'll give you a nod when they arrive. They're in most nights when they aren't on duty so they shouldn't be too long."

The two men thanked Mick and found places at one of the tables where they could see the owner and be ready for his signal. It also gave them a good view of the door and of all of those who entered. It was over an hour later that three men swaggered into the room wearing their reddish-brown woollen coats but minus any armour. It was not easy to enjoy yourself when not on duty wearing armour so most soldiers left their breastplates and helmets at their lodgings.

One of them, a big man with broad shoulders indicated to a group at one table to move so that they could sit. Not wanting any trouble from the big man they moved to another table without any argument. Once vacated the three of them sat down and waved to the owner to bring them drink. The owner nodded in acknowledgement and also to James and Daniel that these were the men he thought they were looking for.

As Daniels watched the three men his stomach tightened into a knot. He instinctively knew that these were the men he was looking for, but he had to be sure, he had to get close and get them talking about themselves.

Telling James to stay where he was Daniel moved to the table where the three men were seated.

"Gentlemen," he addressed them. "Might an ex-soldier buy three serving soldiers a drink?"

They viewed him suspiciously and with a contentious look. They were not used to strangers buying them a drink.

Daniel sat down without being asked and waved at Mick to bring some drinks.

"And who might you be?" asked the big man. "Ex-soldier you say. Who did you fight for then? The Queen of Sheba." He added mockingly.

The man's two companions laughed at the big man's joke.

"I fought for Cromwell of course." Lied Daniel. "I fought at many a place for him. "Marston Moor was my last fight where my horse threw me and I damaged my back. I can't ride for any distance any more so had to leave the service. But I'm always happy to share a glass or two with those that still serve." The lies were coming a bit easier.

"My name is Daniel and I'm here looking for premises that I can rent. And who are you gentlemen that I might address?" he asked

"My names Nathan and my friend here is Benjamin and this is the Capt'n. Captain Jeremiah Hopkins that is, who I'm sure you must have heard of."
"Oh I certainly have" Daniel thought to himself, grateful that his search was over and that justice can now finally be done.
Mick placed four fresh tankards on the table and returned to his place near to the kegs.

"Here's to Ironsides." said Daniel lifting his tankard and giving the Roundheads toast. The three men joined in, Daniel it seemed had been accepted into the company.
"Have you been in Newcastle for very long?" he asked them.

"No not that long, six or seven weeks now. We came over from Carlisle after it fell to the Scots. We have a good billet not far from here so we're hoping to stay here for a while amongst all of these eager women." One of them replied waving his hand around at the boisterous room.

"That's a coincidence," said Daniel, "I travelled from there last week. I had to break my journey though and stayed overnight at Hexham to rest my back."

"Oh we stayed there overnight as well. I hope that you enjoyed your stay as much as we did." said the other man with a smirk. "We stayed with a woman said she was married and that her husband would be home soon. But she must have been lying because he never turned up."

The three of them laughed as they looked at each other.

"The Captain done her proud though didn't you Capt'n?" The smaller man said.

"I gave her what she was asking for." The big man stated. "It was obvious what she wanted. I gave her just a little bit of persuasion to help her get it. It was all going well until that old man came in and spoiled it. Made my fist all bloody he did."

The three soldiers laughed louder and longer this time while Daniel pretended to be drinking his Ale. Inside of him the anger was building up and he knew that he must get away from them before it showed. Finishing his drink he bade them 'well' and left closely followed by James who had been watching the scene as it had been played out.

"Well," James asked, "is it them?"

"Aye it's them alright. I had to get out of there before I lost my temper and nearly spoiled what I have planned for them. Anyway you go on home James. I'm going to wait here and follow them when they leave. I want to find out where they're staying. I don't want to lose track of them now that we've found them. I'll be back later on."

Daniel found a spot where he could see the entrance to Mucky Micks without being seen himself. He had a long wait but eventually as the night wore on and lanterns were lit to give some light to those on the street the three men appeared at the doorway.

The big man led the way with his arm around a woman while the other two followed on.

 Daniel followed them at a safe distance making sure that the Roundheads did not spot him but it was obvious they were more interested in the woman than anything else. They eventually arrived at their lodgings near to the town walls where Daniel carefully noted the house's location before returning to the Sandgate and James and Charlie.

Over the next few days Daniel familiarised himself with the area around Mucky Micks and the house where he had seen the Roundheads enter.

One thing he was sure of is that he couldn't take on the three of them at once and win it would have to be one at a time. He wanted to save the big man until last to make him suffer so he began to make his plans accordingly

Chapter 16

Justice is Served

It was late in the evening when he left the house in Sandgate with the crossbow concealed beneath his cloak. Instead of using the Pandon Gate where he might be recognized or stopped by the guards he choose instead to creep through one of the breeches in the town walls that had been made by the Scots the previous year.

Once inside the walls he made for Mucky Micks to check that the Roundheads were inside. If not he would try again another night. Making sure that he was not seen he peered through the doorway and sure enough sat at their usual table were the three soldiers.

Daniel had chosen a place where the soldiers would pass on their way back to their lodgings. It was on a corner that was lit by a lantern that gave off enough light that should be adequate for his purpose. As the Roundheads would turn the corner he would shoot the shortest of them and if he had time the next one. The only problem he had was the time that it would take to reload the crossbow.

Moving into the shadows he began preparing the crossbow for the first shot. Standing the crossbow upright onto the D shaped ring at the end, he put one foot through the ring and then placing the draw string onto a hook on his belt he straightened both of his legs drawing the string back until he could place it onto the trigger mechanism. Freeing the string from the hook on his belt he loaded one of the special bolts that Alan's father had made for him. The bolt was heavy, made so because of the full bladed sharpened steel head that would piece metal if required. He slid the bolt into the grove on the crossbow shaft and positioned it onto the string and settled down to wait.

It was very quiet with no other people about so he heard the cursing and drunken laughter before he saw them appear from around the corner. He held the crossbow ready and once he was sure of his target gently squeezed the trigger. The heavy bolt flew swift and sure and found its target in the lower abdomen of Nathan slicing through the skin and intestines before coming to a stop jammed between the vertebrae of his spine. On impact Nathan had stepped backwards before falling to his knees. His two companions looked down at him with some amazement at the bolt protruding from his body, which he now held in both hands not quite sure himself what had happened.

As realization reached their drunken minds the two stepped back into the shadows and then turned and ran off in the direction that they had come from leaving Nathan where he was.

Daniel strode forward to confront Nathan. He wanted him to know who had done this to him and why. He reached the sobbing man and grabbing a handful of his hair pulled his head back so that he could look into his face.

"This is for the fun that you had in Hexham when you and your friends raped my wife and for beating a harmless old man, who was my father and died because of it. I doubt you'll be troubling anyone else in the same way again. But I haven't finished with you yet."

Just then he heard the sound of several running footsteps coming towards them. The other two must have alerted the town guards for help.
Stepping backwards Daniel drew his knife from its scabbard and still holding back the kneeling man's head he cut deeply into Nathan's throat, severing his windpipe and sending blood spurting from the wound.
It was not how he wanted to finish punishing the man but it would have to do. Picking up the crossbow he slipped back into the shadows and retraced his way back to James's house in the Sandgate.

It was over a week later that the 'Newcastle News,' a local Broadsheet, appeared listing the brutal slaying of one of Cromwell's brave soldiers and quoting that a reward would be paid for anyone offering information to the capture of the assassin.

Meanwhile Daniel had not been wasting any time in planning for quarry number two. He had noticed that the soldiers did not visit Mucky Micks every night because they had duties to fulfil. After watching their accommodation he followed them to the town wall where they would patrol certain lengths that they had been allocated to guard.

Newcastle before the Scots occupation had become a prosperous town with coal and animal exports and foreign imports and trading established around the country. Because many people had moved into the town to share in its wealth, along with a natural rising population it was not surprising that accommodation had become scarce. Every bit of spare ground within the walls had been built upon with some of the houses erected within an arm's length of the walls.

Daniel had noticed that one such house was close to the part of the wall patrolled by the second Roundhead, Benjamin. He made enquiries and discovered that the house was unoccupied; the occupant was away visiting her sister on the other side of the river. Her husband was dead. He had been killed in the previous year's fighting defending the town against the Scots.

The wall of the house facing the town wall had an upstairs window that was just slightly higher than where a patrolling soldier would pass and close enough to reach out and touch him. This would do nicely.

One evening once it was dark, Daniel forced entry into the house carrying a length of rope and a stout length of timber. He left them in the upstairs room and closed up the forced door. He would return when Benjamin was on duty.

It was not until the following week that Benjamin made his way to the Newgate and reported for duty. Daniel had followed him and took up position in the house by the wall and waited.

It was boring doing guard duty; Benjamin had to patrol between two towers that took him approximately ten minutes to walk one way. He would vary his pace just to relieve the boredom and wonder what the Capt'n had lined up for their next night out. He thought about Nathan. It was a pity that he was gone, he was good fun to be with and he wondered why someone had done that to him. Lost in thought he patrolled between the towers.

Daniel waited until the light was nearly fading and then made his move. He quietly opened the window and positioning the timber across each side of the window frame he tied one end of the rope to it allowing enough length to reach to the town wall and made a running noose at the other end.

As Benjamin passed below the window Daniel dropped the noose around his neck and quickly jerked it back, tightening the noose causing the Roundhead to step backwards into space. Benjamin slammed backwards into the wall of the house with both of his hands clawing at the rope that was closing his windpipe and preventing him from calling out. Daniel slowly let out the rope lowering Benjamin until he was left dangling with his only his tiptoes on the ground. Securing the rope Daniel made his way out of the house to confront Benjamin who was gasping for breath and swaying from side to side as he tried to find a foothold so that he could relieve the pressure on his throat.

Daniel stood in front of the swaying man so that he could see who was doing this to him.
"The law states that anyone found guilty of rape or murder shall suffer a just punishment. Normally the people would sentence that the guilty would be hung and castrated as their punishment. As a soldier of Cromwell you probably consider yourself above the law.

Well you are not. By your own admission you are guilty of the crimes of raping my wife and beating an old man, my father, to death and I am here to administer the punishments."

Drawing his knife Daniel moved close to Benjamin and avoiding the kicks from Benjamin's legs cut open his trousers, and quickly but clumsily castrated him. He then sliced open his stomach allowing his intestines to spill out. Benjamin's scream was trapped in his throat by the rough rope around his neck as he struggled to hold in his intestines with one hand and at the same time relieve the pressure on his windpipe with the other.

Stepping back from the gushing blood spilling around his feet Daniel spoke to the hanging man.

"Justice has been done. You will hope that the rope does its job as you weaken or that you bleed out before the town dogs get the scent of your blood." And turning away he left the man to his fate.

The following week's edition of the "Newcastle News' gave a full description of the second brutal killing of one of Cromwell's soldiers. It went on to inform everyone that:-

"as this is the second such killing of one of Cromwell's soldiers the authorities are concerned that there may be a Royalist gang intent on causing unrest amongst the people and the authorities by such actions. The people of Newcastle are reminded that a substantial reward is being offered for information leading to the arrest of the perpetrators. If such slayings continue then the authorities would have no option but to take drastic measures to prevent any further occurrence of such deeds."

The people of Newcastle were not really bothered about the loss of another of Cromwell's soldiers, in fact they wished they were all gone along with their Scottish allies and that they were left in peace to get on with their lives. But the threat of drastic measures made them all feel uneasy because this usually meant hostages would be randomly seized and executed in a similar fashion as the victim.

The days began to get shorter as the nights closed in. The wind blowing down the river began to have an icy bite to it. Daniel was trying to work out a way to deal with the third and final soldier. It wouldn't be easy as the Captain would be on his guard after the slaying of his two companions. He discussed this with James asking him if he had any ideas on how to go about it.

"Depends what you have in mind for him?" James asked.

"What I would prefer would be to have him pegged out there on Journeys End so that he would know what was coming to him and that he had no escape. That's what I would really want." replied Daniel. "But it would be difficult getting him out there without causing a bit of a kerfuffle and attracting unwanted attention."

"There may be a way." said James thoughtfully. "You say that he enjoys women and likes to hurt them. If you were to tell him that you know someone across the river that will do anything for him for a few pennies that may be a way of getting him to the water."

"I doubt it." answered Daniel "He's not stupid and would probably be suspicious if I told him that."

"But what if he was drunk? He might believe you then."

"He doesn't get drunk at least I've never seen him drunk." James stood up and went over to the oak dresser where most of the cooking utensils and plates were stored. Reaching up to the top cupboard he lifted down a small jar.

"I went to visit my brother a few years ago hadn't seen him for a good while, he's living up in Edinburgh." James returned to the table and placed the jar upon it.

"I travelled up the old Roman road," he continued, "Deere Street I think they used to call it, anyway I got caught in a bad snowstorm up on Soutra Hill. I thought that I'd had it, couldn't see a hand in front of me. Lucky for me though I stumbled across the old Infirmary that the monks used to run. Been there for hundreds of years but the family that owns the ground wanted it shut down. Anyway I got inside out of the elements and was met by a solidary old monk. I think he was the last of them. He made me welcome and gave me hot food and drink. The storm continued for nigh on a week so me and the old monk had plenty of time to talk. I think he was pleased to have my company and he told me many things mainly about medicine."

James tapped the jar on the table.
"He gave me this and said that if ever I had to put someone to sleep, then just give them a small portion of this. They gave it to those if they had to carry out an amputation. It's a powder they made from Opium, Hemlock and something else, I can't remember what it was now, mustn't give too much though otherwise they would never wake up. If you could slip some of this into his drink it would make him drowsy then we could get him down to the river. What do you think?"

"I think that's the best idea yet, I should have thought of something like that." Replied Daniel, "But what do you mean 'we'? I don't want to get you involved in case there's any problem."

"You'll not manage by yourself or even the both of us. I'll have a word with Billy and Mattie see if they'll give a hand as well. We want to do this proper and leave no trace of him that can bring any blame to the town. If we do it right it will be suspected that he has deserted to the Royalist."

Daniel began to protest but James held up his hands. Subject closed. After James had spoken with his crewmen and obtained their agreement to help all that remained was to decide when. Daniel insisted that it had to be when the tide was on the ebb so that Hopkins would have the full six hours before the tide turned again. That would give him plenty of time to reflect on why he was in this position and it had to take place in the evening or at night when Hopkins would be at Mucky Micks. James didn't think that the tide would be suitable at the right time until a few weeks' time so they had ample time for planning.

It was a late afternoon when the day's work was over and James was mooring up the Keelboat that a voice shouted over that someone was waiting in the Quayside Tavern that wanted to speak with Daniel.

Not expecting anyone and having no idea who it could be Daniel was careful in approaching the Tavern. Had he been found out somehow and could this be a trap? As he approached there was no obvious sign of soldiers and only a solidary horse outside hitched to the tethering ring on the wall. Stepping inside it was busy with other Keelmen who had finished work and were slaking their thirst. In one corner sat a young man about sixteen years old staring somewhat fearfully at the rough looking Keelmen around him. Daniel walked over and confronted him.

"I believe that you might be looking for me." And he told him his name.

"I am indeed sir." answered the boy, "Mr Horsley, the Blacksmith sent me with a message saying that you should return with all haste. He said that I should ask on the Quayside for you. I'm pleased that I've found you sir."
"What is it? What's the problem?" Daniel asked the boy.

"I've no idea sir. He just said to find you and say that you should return with all haste." The boy repeated.
Daniel's mind was in a whirl, what could be the matter that he had to return with haste. It was too late in the day to set off now. The road would be dark before he got half way, the horse could easily

trip on the uneven surface and damage a leg; best wait for morning and set off at first light.

"Come with me." He told the boy and he took him to the stables where his horse was looked after. Making arrangements with the owner he told the boy he could stable his horse and sleep here for the night and return to Hexham with him in the morning.

He then went to find James and Charlie to tell them what the boy had said.

"You'll have to go." said Charlie although she did not want him to. "Perhaps your wife or your children are not well. You would only worry if you didn't."

James agreed. They would put plans on hold until he returned and in the meanwhile he would organise a discreet watch on Hopkins so that they knew of his whereabouts.

Daniel and the boy set off at first light but did not arrive at Hexham until mid-morning. It had rained quite heavily during the night; holes in the road were filled with water some of them quite deep and the muddy surface made the going quite difficult for the horses. If they had travelled during darkness anything could have happened.

Tired and spattered with mud they arrived outside of Daniel's house to be met by Denise's sister, Alice, who was accompanied by an old lady.

Daniel dismounted and made for the doorway but Alice blocked his way.

"I'm sorry Daniel you've arrived too late. Denise passed away during the night. She started her labour two days ago. I wanted to send for you straight away but Denise said to wait. When it was obvious that things weren't right I asked Andrew to send a boy with a message for you to come straight away. Agnes here was looking after Denise; she has delivered many babies," Alice gestured to the old lady who acted as the village midwife; "she did her best but couldn't save her."

The old lady stepped forward, "The baby was the wrong way round and I couldn't get it turned. The cord became wrapped around the baby's neck and I couldn't free it. It gave up. Your wife was very tired and in pain, exhausted she was and I think her heart gave out; she just leant back and was gone. I'm very sorry I couldn't save her."

"Where is she?" he asked.

"We've laid her out inside." Alice answered

"And the children where's Tom and Elizabeth?" Daniel asked

"They're over at my house. I thought it best if they stayed with me." Alice told him.

Daniel entered the house and saw that they had laid Denise out on the table. They had washed her and dressed her in a clean dress and she looked very peaceful as if she was sleeping. He stayed beside his wife for a while remembering the times that they had enjoyed before he left to fight for the King. The thoughts of how this had come about flooded into his mind along with the anger in his heart. He would make the remaining Roundhead suffer for what he had done. He turned and left the two women to wrap Denise in her shroud.

After the funeral Daniel stayed with the children for a few weeks and then the urge to get on and finish the business with the one remaining Roundhead became too strong and he made plans to return to Newcastle. But before he left he visited Andrew at the Blacksmiths and returned the crossbow. He thanked him and told him that he had made good use of it and asked if there was any news of Alan but Andrew had given up hope of hearing from his son again.

Alice had agreed that the children could stay with her until things got sorted out; she would take care of them and see that they were fed and clothed; after all they were her sister's children.

It was with mixed feelings that Daniel returned to Newcastle. Denise's death had left him feeling empty knowing that something and everything would never be the same again. But he admitted to himself that he was looking forward to being with Charlie again and hearing her laughter and felt some guilt at his thoughts. He would have to get something organised about the children. Should he return to Hexham or should he start afresh in Newcastle with them. He couldn't think straight but he was determined on one thing and that was to finish the business with the Roundhead before he decided on anything.

Charlie and James were pleased to see him return and even Sam the dog gave him a friendly bark of greetings. They were impatient for his news but waited until he had stabled his horse and unpacked his few belongings.
He told them about Denise and what had happened and how he blamed it all on the actions of the three Roundheads.

"Is the Captain of them still here?" he asked James.

"Aye." He replied, "Don't worry we've kept an eye on him since you've been away. I've been busy with a few other things as well. I know where he stables his horse and there's an old woman that keeps their lodgings tidy and does a bit of cooking for him. She would be prepared to help by passing us his armour and personal things while he was out. We don't want any repercussions on the townsfolk so we have to make it appear as if he's left of his own accord."

Daniel had forgotten about the veiled threat in the 'Newcastle News', but James hadn't.

"Have you discovered when the tides would be right so that we can decide upon a date?" He asked.

"I have," answered James "There's such a tide in three days' time along with a full moon. The next one wouldn't be until next month so we have to decide now and make sure that the Captain will be at Mucky Micks."
Charlie did not want to be involved or know anything about their plans so had left them to go and get fresh food for their evening meal.

It was three days later that the four men gathered in James's house to put their plan into action.

They would wait at a distance from Mucky Micks until they saw the Captain arrive. Once he was inside and settled Daniel would enter engage him in conversation and ensure that he stayed while Billy would hurry to the accommodation and collect the armour and belongings from the old lady and take them down to where they had moored a rowing boat down at the Quayside. Mattie would take the Captain's horse to another stable until it could be moved somewhere far away from the town. James would wait for them outside until they returned and then the three would enter together so the Daniel would know that all was well.

Hopkins recognised Daniel as he entered as Daniel gave him a friendly wave before collecting a drink and joining him at his table.

"How are you Capt'n?" Daniel asked "I haven't seen you for a while now. In good health I hope. Where are your two friends? Are they not with you tonight?"

Hopkins gave Daniel his usual unfriendly glare but was pleased that he had someone that he knew to talk with.

"Murdered, both of them they are. But that's to be expected here in the barbaric north. And where have you been?" Hopkins asked.

"I'm just back from visiting someone I met in Hexham." Daniel replied. Hoping that his mention of Hexham might plant a thought in the big man's brain and remind him of what he had done there.

Hopkins grunted a mumbled reply saying "There's not much there, was glad to leave it. Watch my drink will you? Don't want one of this lot stealing it, I'm just going to empty my bladder."

Hopkins stood up and went outside. Across the room James seeing Hopkins leave followed him to check on where he had gone. Daniel seizing the opportunity took a small tin from the pouch on his belt and emptied the white powder into Hopkins Ale and stirred it around with the blade of his knife until none of it remained on the surface. Hopkins returned and resumed his seat facing Daniel.

"Stinks out there just like this place." He laughed.
"Aye it always does. Drink up." Daniel said. "Get the smell and taste out of your throat. It's my turn, I'll get you another."

Hopkins lifted his tankard and drank until it was empty before slamming it down on the table.

"If you insist. I'll have the same again" he replied.

Daniel left and came back with two full tankards of Ale.

"Are you staying here all night?" Hopkins asked

"I'm off over the other side of the river." Daniel replied "I've got directions to a woman over there who will give a man great pleasure for only a few pennies. My friend who told me about her says she's something special."

Daniel could tell that Hopkins was interested straight away.

"Sounds alright does that. What if I came with you, kept you company so as to speak?" he asked
"I'm not sure about that." Replied Daniel "But, well if you really want to you can come with me and try. Let's get some more Ale down us first." He waved over to Mick to bring more Ale. Hopkins began to brag about the women he had been with and Daniel noticed that his speech was becoming slurred and incoherent. His head fell onto his chest at times before he would jerk it upright again.

Daniel signalled over to James to get ready.
"Come on Capt'n lets go and see this woman I was telling you about."

Hopkins tried to stand but couldn't quite make it until he was assisted by Daniel and James who had come across to their table. Mick looked the other way as they left, he didn't want to see anything in case he was asked any questions about Hopkins.

Outside Mattie had a wheel barrow on which they loaded Hopkins who was mumbling away to himself. It would be easier getting him past the guards on the gate if they thought these were just a bunch of Keelmen out getting drunk. The ruse worked and they were soon down by the river and the rowboat. They loaded the semi drugged Hopkins into the boat along with his armour and personal possessions and set off for Journey's End. Once out in the centre of the river they dropped the armour and possessions over the side of the boat; they would never be found in the thick mud of the riverbed, Assisted by the light given off by the full moon and with Mattie and Billy rowing it was easy for James to navigate to the sandbank.

Reaching their destination they made fast the rowboat and dragged Hopkins up to the four stakes set in the mud. Placing him between the stakes they quickly spread-eagled him and secured his hands and feet with strong ropes. The chill from the wet mud on Hopkins back roused him somewhat from his sleep and he opened his eyes wondering where he was. He tried to stand but the ropes holding him down held fast and it finally penetrated his semi-drugged brain that something was not right.

"What's going on?" he asked angrily, "What am I doing here? Let me up."

The four men like avenging angels stood around him looking down at the prostrate figure.

Daniel thanked his three companions for their help and told them that they should leave him and wait by the boat.

Left alone with Hopkins Daniel looked at him with contempt before beginning to speak. Hopkins appeared to look back with puzzlement at why he was here.

"Captain Hopkins you are here because of crimes you have self-admitted to along with two of your fellow companions who are no longer with us and have paid for their part in the crimes. The crimes being the rape of my wife while you were in Hexham and the death of my father."

Realization began to set in with Hopkins, as he understood why he was here. He began to deny his part in what had happened blaming it on the other two but soon realized that he had already bragged about it to Daniel. He fought against the ropes pulling at them but it only served to tighten them more. Giving up he glared at Daniel.

Daniel continued "You are guilty of these crimes and also the death of my wife who died giving birth to your bastard child who obviously didn't want to be on this earth. If you had been tried by the people you would have been found guilty and sentenced to the recognized punishment, hung, drawn and castrated. Sadly we cannot administer all of these punishments here but some we can." Daniel drew his dagger and cut open Hopkins shirt and trousers exposing his bare flesh.

"For the rape and murder of my wife you will suffer castration and death."

Bending down he quickly cut off Hopkins genitalia and placed them on his chest. Hopkins screams could be heard echoing over the empty mud flats.

Daniel continued, "For the murder of my father you will also suffer death but not quickly."

Stopping down he sliced open Hopkins stomach and pulling the flesh apart reached inside and pulled out his intestines, placing the purple mass still attached to Hopkins body alongside the genitalia on his chest. Hopkins screams began fading into chocking sobs.

"You will soon have guests to join you and as you can see there is plenty for them to feast on. Just as soon as the rats smell your blood they will be flocking to join you. I think that before long you will be praying for the tide to come and release you from them."

He turned away from Hopkins and returned to where the others were waiting. Bending down he washed his dagger and hands in the cool water of the river before boarding the boat and then told the others to push clear of Journey's End.

Chapter 17

A Pleasant Surprise

The following month Daniel left for Hexham this time accompanied by Charlie. He wanted her to meet the children and Denise's sister Alice. He also had some arrangements to make with the girls who were still producing leather goods that he had an outlet for in Newcastle.

The children were always pleased to see their father but they weren't sure about Charlie. They wanted to know why she had a boy's name but when she said that they could call her Claire they said that was better name and began showing her around the village. It didn't take long for them to accept Claire into their lives or for Claire to relieve Alice with a welcome break by taking on the natural care that only women can provide in looking after children.

It was not very long before the children asked Daniel if Claire was to be their new mother and would she be staying with them.

"Would you like her to be?" Daniel asked them.

"Oh yes please." they replied, "Aunt Alice is very kind to us but Claire is a little kinder."

Daniel chuckled at the children's logic and told them that they would have to wait and see. He later told Claire what they had said and asked her what she thought.

"About what?" she asked smiling "Being their mother."

"Yes," Daniel replied, "but you couldn't be a proper mother unless we were married, could you?"

"I suppose not." she replied "But you haven't asked me if I would marry you have you? Or is this a proposal?" purposely making him feel awkward.

"Well yes I suppose it is. Claire, I mean Charlie will you marry me? He blurted out.

"Of course I will." And laughing they held each other tight.

Before returning to Newcastle Daniel explained to the children that as soon as he managed to organise things they would all be together but in the meantime they would remain with Alice.

Alice was happy for the children to stay with her for the time being for she knew that Daniel had to get things organised first of all.

He left some money for the girls who were making the leather goods but also told them to produce some men's shirts and undergarments. He would take them back with him after his next visit. He had one more call to make and that was to a shepherd that lived out on the Northumberland moors. On his previous visit he had asked him to make a coat of sheepskin for Claire and was now on his way to collect it. It would keep her nice and warm during the cold winter months. Claire who was now used to being called Claire, and was beginning to prefer it, loved the coat and wore it all of the way back to Newcastle.

James was in the doorway to the house when they arrived back and greeted them most warmly for he had missed them around the house.
"It's good to see you both back safe and sound and I've tided up the house Charlie so you won't have to bother."

"I would prefer it if you called me by my proper name father," Claire replied "and not that boyish name that you've always called me."
James was taken aback, stunned for a moment you might say.

239

"And what would that proper name be, may I ask?" James asked raising his eyebrows.

"Why it's Claire of course." And she turned and entered the house.

James shook his head as he picked up her valise and was heard to mutter, "Women!"

From that moment on Charlie became Claire.

Just as soon as they had unpacked, Daniel asked James if he could speak to him on a serious matter. Claire pretended to be busy doing some small task on the other side of the room but remained discreetly within earshot.

"James" Daniel began, "I would be most beholden to you if you would give permission for Claire and me to be married."

James looked at him and hesitated for a short while before replying.
"Married you say. How do you propose to support her? You have no regular means of providing for her that I know of. What will you do for money?"

Inside himself James was more than happy that Daniel had asked for his permission and he knew that his answer would be yes. But he did feel obliged to ask what Daniels future plans were. Claire had stopped pretending to work and was glaring at her father who very wisely ignored her stares.

"I do have some plans for the future." Daniel answered, "Before I went to fight for the King I used to bring goods from Hexham to some of the traders here. It provided for a modest income but I thought what if I traded here myself and cut out the middleman it would provide enough for me to support a wife as well. I would of course require accommodation for the goods and somewhere to trade from but I'm sure that can be arranged."

Both Claire and her father listened as Daniel explained his plans because he had never mentioned them to either of them before.

James interrupted Daniel "Enough, enough. Of course you have my permission. I would be more than pleased to have you in the family as my son in law. Now, have you set a date because I'm sure the two of you have been planning this for a while? Am I right?"

They all laughed when it was agreed that they had spoken about it.

It was agreed that the wedding would take place just as soon as all of the arrangements could be made'

In the meanwhile Daniel would continue to help out on the Keelboat while Claire remained to look after the house and have meals ready for the two men when they returned from work.

On his first trip down the river to the colliers' moored in deeper water Daniel was determined not to look at where they had pegged out Hopkins. However as they passed by 'Journeys End' his eyes were drawn to where the four posts could be seen. There was nothing to see, the rats had done their job and the tide had done the rest carrying what was left out to sea.

Cromwell had imposed his puritan beliefs on all of the country decreeing that there was to be no pointless enjoyment including singing, unless it was hymns and no dancing and that people dress in plain clothes, drab most folk would say. The Roundhead soldiers imposed enforcement of these puritan standards with strict punishment for offenders.

However this was Newcastle governed by the Scottish victors who had taken the town. Cromwell's ideas of how the people should live their lives did not go down well with the townsfolk or by the Scots who enjoyed the sound of the bagpipes and a good Scottish

Ceilidh. So Cromwell's ideas were not entirely enforced, especially so when it involved the Keelmen.

The wedding took place in St Hilda's Mission a small church used by the Keelmen just outside the town walls and the celebrations at the Keel Inn at the far end of the Quayside where most of the Keelmen gathered for a drink and to socialise.

Lots of people attended the wedding before making their way down to the Quayside including some townsfolk who had been invited by friends in the Keelmen's families. A small band played various tunes on the Northumberland Pipes and a squeezebox as the people danced around the Quay. Later everyone was surprised when some off duty Scottish soldiers arrived and joined in the festivities by playing their bagpipes to the enjoyment of the crowd. They entertained the folk with displays of sword dancing and Scottish Reels and also joined in dancing with the locals in the Northumberland Reels.

As the afternoon turned to evening the wind blowing down the river turned cold and Claire left to put on her sheepskin coat that Daniel had given her. When she returned she received many admiring glances and many requests from other ladies about where had she got her coat from?

"You'll have to ask my husband." She told them "He has someone who makes them for him."

For the rest of the evening Daniel was inundated with requests from men whose wives insisted they needed a coat just the same as Claire's. Daniel promised he would do his best to oblige all of them but that it might take some time before they received the coats; the list was quite long. No matter they all answered get the coats so as we get some peace.

This was the opening that Daniel was after. He would get the shepherd who made the coat to start making more and to employ some of the village women to help him produce the coats as quickly as possible. He would pay them a fair wage and a little more if they produced them quickly. He left a few days later for Hexham to get things organised.

Within the next couple of months Daniel had supplied all of those that had requested a sheepskin coat. One of his contacts on the Quayside who ran a Ships Chandler's had allowed him to use part of his warehouse to store any excess coats for a small price. It would have to do for the time being until he had enough funds to get his own building.

As time went on word of his goods spread and business was good. Soon he had acquired his own premises on the Quayside and had added to his stock with leather jackets and jerkins made by the same staff in Hexham. He also stocked a large selection of swords and daggers and some items of armour made by Alan's father. The shop was well situated because not only did townsfolk visit it but also seamen from the many ships using the river. One of the captains from a ship enquired if he had any clothing that would shed water when he was caught in a storm. While the answer was no it made Daniel think that it should be possible. He acquired some old sailcloth from one of his visitors that he made into long coats that he experimented on by treating them with linseed oil that appeared to work and kept the wearer fairly dry.

With business improving the next step was to build a house for Claire and to bring the two children to live with them. There would also be room for James to move in with them as he was not getting any younger and would before long have to give up skippering a Keelboat. It was likely he would recommend to the owners that Mattie or Billy replace him as skipper of the Keelboat.

It was just over a year from when he had moved to Newcastle that the Scottish army moved out of the town and marched back over the Border to Scotland. The King had formed an agreement with the Scottish Covenanters and established their support. The Scots made a fine sight as they left the town with Bagpipes playing and drums beating and many a townsfolk were sorry to see them leave as they had made friends with many of the soldiers.

With the leaving of the Scots, Newcastle Corporation had to reform and establish a new Board of Trade along with new Committees and new members to replace those that had been killed resisting the Scots. Now that Daniel was a recognized successful businessman he was offered a seat on several of these.

These were still troubled times the King and Parliament were still at war with each other and battles were still being fought. But before the decade was out news that Parliament had executed the King shocked all of the people no matter which side they fought on. With Cromwell now as the self-proclaimed Lord Protector the unwelcome chains of Puritanism were heavily imposed on all of the population. This was to last for a further decade until Cromwell's death and the return of the monarchy which pleased the population that was tired of Puritan ways. Charles II was welcomed back as King of England.

Daniel had managed to weather life under Cromwell and keep control of his business as well as looking after those who worked for him. He was not alone in rejoicing when news of King Charles II return to England filtered through from London. Parties and celebrations went on for days as the people let their hair down after being restricted for so long.

It was during this time that Alan's father Andrew, who was now quite elderly, sent for Daniel and that he should be prepared for a pleasant surprise.

Wondering what it could be Daniel set off for Hexham leaving behind Claire and the three children. Claire in the previous year had given birth and they now had a second girl in the family.

Nearing Andrew's house and the forge Daniel heard the loud hammering of someone busy working in the forge. Dismounting he entered the building and couldn't believe what he was seeing.

There at the anvil hammering away at a horseshoe was Alan, his old comrade in arms.

"Alan," he cried out, "Alan is that really you?"

Alan turned surprised by Daniel's shout." Daniel! I never thought to see you again." Laying down his hammer he moved to greet his friend.

The two of them threw their arms around each other in a manly embrace.

"Where have you been?" Daniel asked his friend

"I've no idea." Alan replied "All that I remember is riding away from Naseby and then we must have become separated and that's it. The next thing was that I found myself as naked as the day that I was born here in the Forge. I must have hit my head or something and lost my memory and found my way here somehow. Where have you been?"

"It's a long story and I've much to tell you but we can catch up later." Daniel replied

Alan's father walked into the forge smiling "I thought that I would give you a surprise." He said "I didn't want to spoil it by telling you the news. My prayers have been answered and I have my son back again before I die."

"This calls for a celebration." said Daniel smiling "Come on let's go and have some Ale. The Tavern is quite near."

As the three of them left the forge, from across the road a tall old man dressed in a dark cloak, his face concealed by a long beard and with grey hair protruding from under a leather skullcap, watched the scene with some satisfaction.
"It was good to see two good friends reunited," thought Merlin, as he turned and walked away into the Mists of Time.

Epilogue
Updates

Daniel Colbert: Royalist volunteer and soldier of King Charles I.

Denise Colbert, Daniels wife: Denise had waited patiently for the return of her husband from the Civil War always believing that he would one day return. Her patience was rewarded with Daniels return and she took great pleasure in showing him his three year old son and six year old daughter.

Mark McDade: Long term member of the Security Services. In recognition of the part he played in the downfall of the RGB Mark was promoted to Northern Area Controller. He resigned his position with the Sealed Knot Society and now uses his activities as a businessman as cover for his Security Services activities.

Kathleen McDade: Because of Mark's increasingly periods of absence due to his work commitments Kath pressurised Mark to sell the large house and move into a smaller flat nearer to her daughters where she can be closer to them and the grandchildren.

Claire McDade, Daughter of Mark McDade: Gave birth to Daniel's baby boy who she also christened Daniel after his father.

Each year a substantial sum of money was deposited into her bank account from an unknown benefactor in recognition of her partner saving the life of the King. At the time of writing she has neither married or is with a new partner. She is now a senior lecturer at Newcastle University and a recognised authority on the life and times of the English Civil Wars.

Alan Horsley: Royalist volunteer and soldier of King Charles I.

Maureen McDade: Daughter of Mark McDade

Alan and Maureen were married and raised a family of two boys and a girl. Mark had recommended that Alan be recruited into the Security Services where he enjoyed a successful career for ten years. However while following a known terrorist he was involved in a high-speed car pursuit. While swerving to avoid some pedestrians his car skidded and crashed, bursting into flames. It is believed that because of the intensity of the flames no remains were recovered from the wreckage.

Jerimiah Hopkins: Officer in Cromwell's New Model Army.

Benjamin Castle: Soldier in Cromwell's New Model Army.

Nathan Levin: Soldier in Cromwell's New Model Army

Of the three Roundhead soldiers in Part Two, nothing more was seen or heard of them only the clothes that they had been wearing were found and they were listed as some of the 186,000 British people that are reported missing each year.

Regarding the three soldiers of the same name in Part Three, it was widely rumoured that the officer may have planned their murder when they refused to desert to the Royalists along with him.

Richard Fox and James Radcliffe: were both placed on trial for Treason and High Treason and attempted murder. They were sentenced to life imprisonment to serve with a minimum of thirty years before being considered for parole.

Edward Okey: After investigation he was found not to have assisted in the attempted assassination or have any connection with the RGB. He carried on with his role In the Sealed Knot Society and his visits to the White Bull. It was one evening after a heavy drinking session that he took a stroke while watching the television and died in the ambulance on his way to hospital.

Gerry Marshall: No connection was established with the RGB and he continues with his business of selling and restoring Antique weapons.

Craig Adams: Craig's name and his association with the RGB were discovered on the Laptop held by Ian Blacklock. The Police raided his house in the early hours of the morning but Craig was out. It is believed that a neighbour may have phoned Craig and warned him of the Police raid because he has not returned to his house or reported for work at the nightclub. His details have been placed on the National Police Watch List but so far no trace of him has been reported

Leroy Walter Kitelinger: Took early retirement on sick grounds. He suspected that his involvement in supplying the gun used in the attempted assassination would eventually become known or at least the CIA would want to know what happened to one of their rifles. He visited Switzerland and opened a Bank Account at one of the leading banks. On returning to England he emptied his own account with the British Bank and transferred the money to his Swiss account. He did the same with the several accounts that he had opened under a fictitious name where he had stowed the proceeds from his Drug dealing activities. Leroy then disappeared. He had left instructions with his Swiss bank that on receipt of a pre-agreed coded message from him, they were to transfer an amount stipulated in the message via Western Union to a given location. The last trace that the CIA had led them to Lima in Peru, but by the time they had a team arrive there they were too late to apprehend Leroy who had moved on.

Len Markam: The Police were very pleased to receive from the Security Services details of his connection with the RGB and of his Drug dealing activities. He was sentenced to serve seven years imprisonment on each charge.

Billy Morrison; for his part in the attempted assassination he was sentenced to fifteen years in prison to be served without remission.

James Ferguson: Was taken to hospital but died as a result of his wounds.

John Greenhead: Sentenced to Eight Years for possession of a firearm and for belonging to the RGB.

Mike Evans: Sentenced to Ten Years imprisonment for RGB membership and possession of a firearm with intent.

Ian Blacklock and Irene Blacklock: Each Sentenced to Five Years imprisonment for money laundering and money lending offences. Ian Blacklock was sentenced to a further five years for belonging to an illegal organisation.

Daniel and Alan: After meeting again in Part Three, the two friends went into partnership with each other spreading their business interest to include building new houses for the increasing population of Newcastle. With the return of King Charles II and the second Civil War their loyalty to the King was tested again and they became involved in subsequent events.

James McDade: Skipper of the Keelboat retired and lived out his life with his daughter Claire, his son in law Daniel and his Granddaughter.

Claire (Charlie) McDade: James's Daughter. Claire's marriage to Daniel was a happy one. She was a good loving wife and bore Daniel a daughter whom they christened Denise. Claire became well known for her involvement in helping out the less fortunate not just in Sandgate but also in the town itself.

Mattie Robson: Before retiring James recommended to the Keelboat's owners that Mattie took over as skipper of the Keelboat. He told them that Mattie knew the river as well as he did and that their boat would be in safe hands. His recommendation was accepted and Mattie took over as Skipper of the Keel.

Billy Johnson: Billy suffered a serious accident while spreading coal in the Keelboat's hold. The man responsible for releasing the coal from the coal stack chute did not check before releasing a load. Billy was standing under the coal when it fell and suffered a broken shoulder and arm, cuts to the head and severe concussion.

As a result of the accident Billy was no longer able to work on the Keelboat or provide for his family. On hearing of the accident Daniel offered Billy employment in his Quayside store where he spent the rest of his working life happily employed as a storeman.

Merlin: Has appeared several times over the centuries, sometimes under a different name. He has been sighted in France, in Wales, and in Northumberland as a woodcutter and also in Southern Scotland as a Druid. He is best known for the time that he spent at King Arthur's Court as a Magician and an adviser.

Camelot: While many think of Camelot as a mythological place only brought to life in legend there are others who believe that it really existed. Reputed to be the home of King Arthur and his Knights of the Round Table, its location has been known to include *'Chamalot'* as listed in old French manuscripts, in *'Caerleon'* in Wales and in the Scottish Border's where it is said that *Roxburgh Castle* was built on the ruins of Camelot. But perhaps its most widely recognised location is that of *'Tintagel Castle'* in Cornwall. All of these different locations would endorse Merlin's statement in Part One that Camelot is always on the move according to the laws of the Ancients. Does it exist today? Perhaps it does but not as a castle but that of an entity that helps those in need.

Sketch Map of Newcastle Town Walls 1645

(Showing entrance gates and location of James's house and 'Mucky Micks'.)

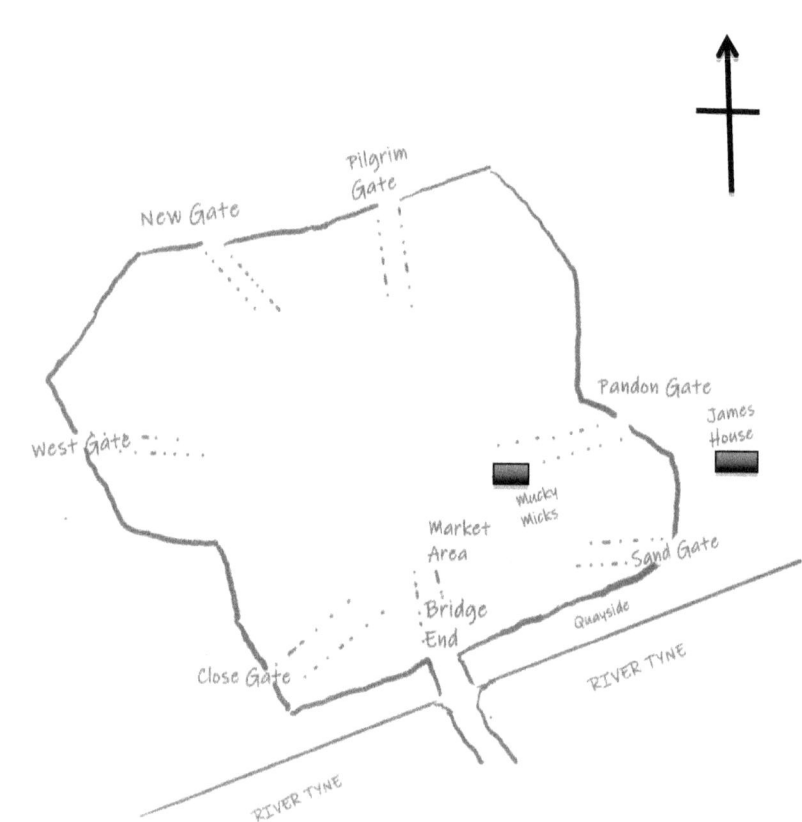

About the Author

David was born and raised in Gateshead an industrial town in the north east of England. He joined the army at the age of eighteen and saw much of his service in Europe and the Middle East. After leaving the army he worked for several years in Nigeria and Saudi Arabia. After returning to the UK he applied to study Information Technology and Data Protection Law. On graduating from his studies he joined the National Health Service where he applied his qualifications in these subjects until his retirement.